Meg,

I've never considered getting married before because I figured it had to involve being in love. As far as I can see, that only causes misery, and I've never gone looking for misery. My dad loved my mom. After she died he grieved for the rest of his life. I've watched friends falling in and out of love, getting married with stars in their eyes then ending up divorced and barely able to speak a civil word to each other. Neither of those situations appeals to me.

But I figure we won't have those problems. We're practical people and our marriage will be a practical arrangement. We'll both be getting out of it what we want without making any emotional demands on each other. I want heirs, and you want children. It's as simple as that.

Zeke

Reluctant Grooms
1. Lazarus Rising
   Anne Stuart
2. A Million Reasons Why
   Ruth Jean Dale
3. Designs on Love
   Gina Wilkins
4. The Nesting Instinct
   Elizabeth August
5. Best Man for the Job
   Dixie Browning
6. Not *His* Wedding!
   Suzanne Simms

Western Weddings
7. The Bridal Price
   Barbara Boswell
8. McCade's Woman
   Rita Rainville
9. Cactus Rose
   Stella Bagwell
10. The Cowboy and the Chauffeur
    Elizabeth August
11. Marriage-Go-Round
    Katherine Ransom
12. September Morning
    Diana Palmer

Instant Families
13. Circumstantial Evidence
    Annette Broadrick
14. Bundle of Joy
    Barbara Bretton
15. McConnell's Bride
    Naomi Horton
16. A Practical Marriage
    Dallas Schulze
17. Love Counts
    Karen Percy
18. Angel and the Saint
    Emilie Richards

Marriage, Inc.
19. Father of the Bride
    Cathy Gillen Thacker
20. Wedding of the Year
    Elda Minger
21. Wedding Eve
    Betsy Johnson
22. Taking a Chance on Love
    Gina Wilkins
23. This Day Forward
    Elizabeth Morris
24. The Perfect Wedding
    Arlene James

Make-Believe Matrimony
25. The Marriage Project
    Lynn Patrick
26. It Happened One Night
    Marie Ferrarella
27. Married?!
    Annette Broadrick
28. In the Line of Duty
    Doreen Roberts
29. Outback Nights
    Emilie Richards
30. Love for Hire
    Jasmine Cresswell

Wanted: Spouse
31. Annie in the Morning
    Curtiss Ann Matlock
32. Mail-Order Mate
    Louella Nelson
33. A Business Arrangement
    Kate Denton
34. Mail Order Man
    Roseanne Williams
35. Silent Sam's Salvation
    Myrna Temte
36. Marry Sunshine
    Anne McAllister

Runaway Brides
37. Runaway Bride
    Karen Leabo
38. Easy Lovin'
    Candace Schuler
39. Madeline's Song
    Stella Bagwell
40. Temporary Temptress
    Christine Rimmer
41. Almost a Bride
    Raye Morgan
42. Strangers No More
    Naomi Horton

Solution: Wedding
43. To Choose a Wife
    Phyllis Halldorson
44. A Most Convenient Marriage
    Suzanne Carey
45. First Comes Marriage
    Debbie Macomber
46. Make-believe Marriage
    Carole Buck
47. Once Upon a Time
    Lucy Gordon
48. Taking Savanah
    Pepper Adams

Please address questions and book requests to: Silhouette Reader Service
U.S.: 3010 Walden Ave., P.O. Box 1325, Buffalo, NY 14269
Canadian: P.O. Box 609, Fort Erie, Ont. L2A 5X3

Reluctant Grooms

ELIZABETH AUGUST

THE NESTING INSTINCT

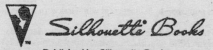

Published by Silhouette Books
America's Publisher of Contemporary Romance

SILHOUETTE BOOKS
300 East 42nd St.,
New York, N.Y. 10017

ISBN 0-373-30104-9

THE NESTING INSTINCT

Copyright © 1990 by Elizabeth August

Celebrity Wedding Certificates published by permission of
Donald Ray Pounders from *Celebrity Wedding Ceremonies*.

This edition published by arrangement with Harlequin Books S.A.

® and TM are trademarks of Harlequin Books S.A., used under license. Trademarks indicated with ® are registered in the United States Patent and Trademark Office, the Canadian Trade Marks Office and in other countries.

Printed in U.S.A.

A Letter from the Author

Dear Reader,

We have all acquired our share of knowledge. For the majority of us, some came from books and some came from life. For others, most came from books or most came from life. Who is to say which is the more important of the lessons or which aids a person more? My mother says that common sense is the most important tool of survival a person can possess. It will keep you out of trouble and lead you in the right direction. Experience causes me to believe she's right.

However, experience has also taught me that a certain amount of formal education is important. In today's world, to succeed to the fullest of one's potential, a person needs to know how to read and write. Zeke Wilson, like many of today's adults, never learned these basic skills. This has not made him less of a person nor stopped him from being a successful farmer. But it has presented difficulties. To me, his decision to seek help makes him a very powerful and admirable character. For a man with his pride and authoritarian demeanor, it isn't easy for him to ask Meg to teach him to read.

As for Meg, I am very familiar with what I've always referred to as "the nesting instinct"...that sudden, strong urge to have children. It has been twenty-five years since my first child was conceived but I can still remember the intense feeling that it was time for me to become a mother. It was as if this was a basic need I had no choice but to fulfill.

I hope you enjoy reading *The Nesting Instinct* as much as I enjoyed writing it. And, I hope you like Meg and Zeke as much as I grew to like them.

Fondly,

Elizabeth August

To my parents, Bettie and Ben,
for teaching me
that a strong, lasting marriage is made,
not born.

Chapter One

"Some days a person just shouldn't get out of bed," Meg Delany declared as she parked in the driveway of the old two-story white frame house she shared with her mother.

Glancing down on the seat beside her, she groaned mentally at the sight of the stack of book reports she had to grade over the weekend. Some days teaching was a joy. Then there were days like today. It was a Friday; it was October and Halloween was near. Secretly she had begun to toy with the idea that fourteen- and fifteen-year-olds actually had little monsters inside them that insisted on coming out periodically. "It would be in keeping with the season," she mused.

As she gathered her books and papers together and climbed out of her car, the sight of the full-sized, four-wheel-drive blue pickup truck in front of the house caused the frown on her face to deepen. In this small Missouri farm town everyone knew everyone else's car on sight, and that pickup belonged to Zeke Wilson.

"What in the world can he be doing here?" she muttered under her breath. While she didn't like admitting that anyone intimidated her, Zeke Wilson did. He was a big man, standing six feet three inches, with broad shoulders and a muscular body that had been developed by years of hard work on his farm. But then, he'd always been big. Although he was two years older than she was, by the time she'd reached fifth grade he'd been held back twice. Because of that, he'd ended up in the same class she was in. But that wasn't because he was dull-witted. Meg and everyone else in town knew that when Zeke Wilson put his mind to a task, that task got done and done well. He just wasn't interested in school. But the law required that every child under the age of sixteen had to attend, and periodically the truant officer would go by the farm and insist that Zeke show up in class for a few days.

He never caused any trouble when he came. He'd just sit in a brooding silence in the back of the room. He wasn't bad-looking. In fact a great many of the girls considered him ruggedly handsome. But he had a way of looking at people with those dark eyes of his that could chill a person to the bone. Once Mrs. James, their fifth-grade teacher, had tried calling on him for an answer, but Zeke had just sat there and stared the woman down. That was the one and only time she tried to get him to participate when he hadn't volunteered on his own. As soon as he turned sixteen, he officially dropped out of school.

After that, his and Meg's paths hadn't crossed much. Meg saw him at church on Sundays, but he never made any move to speak to her or her mother.

So what's he doing here? she wondered again as she went inside through the back door.

"Zeke Wilson's in the parlor waiting for you. *And* he's wearing his Sunday suit," Kate Delany greeted her daughter in a hushed whisper, as Meg entered the kitchen. Kate was short and plump. Her long brown hair, now lightly streaked with gray, was wrapped in a bun on the top of her head. As usual a few wispy strands had escaped, to give her a slightly befuddled appearance. But anyone who looked into her sharp blue eyes knew she didn't miss much. "I offered him some iced tea and when I came back with it, he was pacing around like a caged bear."

Setting the stack of book reports and her briefcase on the table, Meg glanced nervously toward the door.

Kate's gaze followed her daughter's line of vision. "Wonder what he could be wanting?" She said aloud the question Meg had been asking herself since she'd spotted the pickup.

"Guess there's only one way to find out," Meg replied. She told herself that if she could control a room full of active teenagers, she could certainly face Zeke Wilson with equal confidence. But a part of her wasn't convinced.

Leaving the kitchen, she paused in the hall to glance into the mirror. Absently she raked her hands through her short, wavy black hair. The light coating of makeup she wore wasn't doing much to cover the end-of-a-long-day circles under her eyes. Even the color of her eyes looked tired to her. When she'd dressed this morning in the multicolored sweater and trim kelly-green A-line skirt, she could have sworn her eyes matched the green of the skirt. Now they looked almost olive. *Obviously that hazy look I saw on my students' faces today was contagious,* she decided dryly.

You're procrastinating, she chided herself and ordering her feet to move once again, she approached the parlour with Kate following immediately behind.

Zeke was standing staring out the front window. As Meg entered, he turned toward her. He was dressed in his Sunday best, just as her mother had said. His hair, a dark brown in color that matched his eyes, was neatly combed. Even the wayward lock Meg had noticed through the years that seemed to always escape and fall onto his forehead was in place. His expression was polite but not friendly. It was best described as businesslike, she decided, and again wondered what business he could have with her. "Mr. Wilson, what can I do for you?" she asked evenly, matching his manner.

"Miss Delany." His voice had a stiff, formal quality as he acknowledged her presence. Then directing his attention toward her mother, he said, "Mrs. Delany, I don't want to seem rude, but I was wondering if I might speak to your daughter in private?"

Kate glanced toward her Meg hesitantly. The desire to insist that her mother be allowed to remain was strong, but pride made Meg nod toward her in an "it's all right, you can leave" manner.

"Certainly, you may speak to her alone," Kate conceded with a strong edge of disappointment in her voice. Clearly she did not like being left out.

As the door clicked shut behind her mother and Meg found herself alone with Zeke, an uneasiness filled her. He's just a man like any other man, she chided herself. Still the uneasiness persisted. "What can I do for you, Mr. Wilson?" she repeated.

Zeke regarded her grimly. "What I have to say to you is private. I would not like for it to go beyond the two of us. I would prefer to claim that this request is made strictly for business reasons, but that would be a lie. My pride is involved."

Although Meg's curiosity was piqued, she was not certain she wanted to share any secrets with Mr. Zeke Wilson. However she said coolly, "You have my word."

He shifted so that his feet were slightly spread. His stance reminded Meg of an immovable mountain. "I want to hire you to teach me to read."

Her nervousness ruined her control and the surprise this request brought registered on Meg's face. Zeke Wilson was held in high regard by the business community in town. He had a prosperous farm and he was an elder in the church. "You read the Bible passage in church last Sunday," she said in confusion.

"I recited from rote," he corrected. "Joan taught it to me."

Joan, Meg knew, was Joan Oliver. She was an elderly bookkeeper who did accounting and taxes for several of the farmers in the community.

"Joan took care of my dad's accounts when he was alive, and she's been taking care of mine. But she's getting on in age and when she does decide to retire I want to be able to take over my books myself," Zeke elaborated.

Meg studied him narrowly. "You really can't read," she murmured, as if she needed to say it to actually believe it.

"While it's a handicap in many ways, it's not a sin, nor is it uncommon," he pointed out curtly.

"I know. I was just surprised," she said with apology. Her frown of confusion returned. "But I don't understand why you came to me."

"You're an English teacher, aren't you?" he demanded, his scowl deepening.

"Yes, but I don't teach reading," she replied, adding honestly, "I really don't think I'm the person you should have come to. One of the elementary-school teachers would be better suited. I would suggest..."

"Obviously I've made a mistake," he growled, cutting her short. "Sorry I took up your time."

"Mr. Wilson..." she began, but before she could say any more he was gone. She heard his footsteps resounding loudly on the hardwood floor as he strode rapidly down the hall. Then she heard the front door open and close. As the engine of his pickup started and she heard it drive away, Kate came into the study.

"Well, you certainly handled that badly," the older woman said with a reproving frown. "Do you realize what it must have cost that man to come here? He's proud, just like his dad was."

Meg scowled accusingly. "You were eavesdropping."

Kate's shoulders straighted self-righteously. "I was simply standing near the door in case you should need me."

Meg raised a skeptical eyebrow. "Near the door? You must have had your ear pressed against it. You're lucky you weren't trampled when he stormed out of here."

Ignoring her daughter's observations, Kate was shaking her head in a slow, reprimanding manner. "I can't believe you were so insensitive. I thought I'd raised you better than that."

Meg frowned defensively. "I was trying to be reasonable. And his request did come as a shock."

Kate's mouth formed a thoughtful pout. "It makes sense though," she said. "He was around seven or maybe eight when his mother, Sarah, a right pretty woman she was, took sick. It was cancer and by the time they found it, it had spread pretty bad. Doctors said there was nothing they could do to help her. His pa had work around the farm to do, so Zeke would stay at the house to keep an eye on her, fetch her whatever she wanted and all. Several of us volunteered to go sit with her during the day, but that wasn't good enough for Zeke. I've never seen a more determined child. He insisted on staying with his mother in spite of every assurance we gave him that we'd watch over her. I remember Sadie Evans put him on the school bus one morning and the next thing she knew, there he was home again. He'd made the bus driver let him off not more than a quarter of a mile down the road, and he'd walked back. After Sarah died, Zeke started going to school again. But he'd already missed a lot...nearly two years. He's always had an over-abundance of pride. He was probably embarrassed to be so far behind the other kids his age. I remember how he refused to go regular, and his pa was too wrapped up in his own grief to give the boy the guidance he needed. Besides, Pete probably found some solace in having his son with him." Kate nodded vigorously. "I can see how Zeke got behind, and the teachers probably just passed him along because he got too big for the smaller desks."

Meg nodded. She didn't like admitting it, but things like that did happen. Zeke's image filled her mind. He'd behaved unreasonably and his manner had left the impression that as far as he was concerned, he'd never give Meg the time of day again. Then the image of the angry man was replaced by that of a little boy filled with grief. In spite of the fact that she had no desire to face Zeke Wilson again, she knew she couldn't leave things this way. He had asked for her help with a serious matter.

"Well?" Kate demanded. "What are you going to do about Zeke?"

"I'm going to go see him," Meg replied decisively.

But twenty minutes later as she turned into the drive leading to the two-story frame farmhouse, she wasn't feeling as decisive. Half hoping it wouldn't be there, she looked for Zeke's pickup. Luck wasn't with her. She saw it parked in front of the house. "I wonder if this is how Daniel felt when they tossed him into the lion's den," she muttered as she parked near the roofed front porch. Then she scowled at herself in the mirror. She had no reason to be afraid of Zeke Wilson.

Leaving her car, she climbed the steps and knocked on the front door.

"I'm coming!" a male voice growled from inside.

In the next moment the door was jerked open. Zeke had changed from his suit into a pair of old, work-worn jeans and a flannel shirt. The wayward lock of hair was back on his forehead and an unwelcome look was in his eyes.

"You left rather abruptly," Meg said, sounding a great deal calmer than she felt.

"Figured we'd said all there was to say," he replied. "Figure that's still true. Now I've got chores to do, so if you'll excuse me..."

Anger flashed in Meg's eyes. It hadn't been easy coming here, but she'd come. He at least owed her the courtesy of hearing her out! "I still remember the day you stared Mrs. James down in fifth grade. I thought you were the most bullheaded person *I'd* ever seen. Now I've decided you're probably the most bullheaded person in the whole world!"

"She asked me a question she knew I didn't know the answer to," he said with gruff anger. Brushing past Meg, he crossed the porch and started down the steps.

"She just wanted to get you to participate," she pointed out curtly, in defence of the teacher, as she followed behind him.

"I didn't want to participate," he replied dryly, continuing toward the barn without a backward glance.

Meg came to a halt and glared at his retreating back. The urge to leave was strong, but her anger was stronger. He had made her feel guilty and he wasn't going to get away with it. She hadn't refused to help him. She'd just been trying to be reasonable.

She caught up with him as he reached the bar. "Is that how you solve all of your problems . . . you just shut everyone out?" she demanded.

"Yeah, and it usually works just fine," he replied with dismissal.

Meg's hand fastened around his arm. "Well it's not going to work with me." The contact caused a surge of heat to spread from her hand upward through her arm. Unnerved by this acute reaction, she released him abruptly. "You're not going to come into my home and make me feel guilty because I'm trying to be reasonable, then just walk away!" she finished angrily.

The frown on his face deepened. "This isn't your problem."

"You made it my problem when you came to see me." Her gaze narrowed with increased anger. "And that's another explanation you owe me . . . I want to know how come I was so lucky as to be the one you came to!''

"Because you're not married and you're not old," he replied.

She stared at him in confusion. "I don't understand."

He regarded her dryly. "If you were married, you'd have to explain to your husband why you were spending time with me and he'd have to tell his friends so they wouldn't think he was being made a fool of by a fickle wife. If you were too old, then everyone in town would want to know what business I had with you. The busybodies wouldn't stop until they'd found out the truth. I figured that since you weren't married or engaged, people could think I was coming around because I was interested in you. I know you've been seeing Neil Talmage pretty regularly, but he hasn't popped the question yet. Figured it couldn't hurt your chances with him if he thought another man was interested in you. Might make him jealous enough to make a commitment. And you've never been much of a gossip, so I figured you could keep my secret."

Meg had to admit it was a reasonable explanation. But the part about Neil touched a raw nerve. She would never use trickery to get any man to ask her to marry him. Remembering the gossip she'd been hearing lately, she asked with an edge of sarcasm, "Aren't you afraid Rita Gaint might get a little angry?"

"Rita and I are just friends," he answered matter-of-factly.

Meg had to admit that Zeke Wilson did seem to be a confirmed bachelor. Off and on his name had been linked with several women, but in the end he'd always eluded the walk down the aisle. Well, it was probably just as well considering his stubborn disposition, she decided. He'd be impossible to live with. And he'd probably be less than a joy to work with. But she felt trapped. "All right," she said stiffly. "I'll teach you to read. Be at my place at two o'clock on Sunday afternoon."

Then, without giving him a chance to respond, she turned and walked rapidly back toward her car.

Chapter Two

I knew I should have stayed in bed today, Meg
thought with a tired sigh as she drove home. She had
felt Zeke's gaze on her all the way to her car. He made
her uneasy and she didn't appreciate that. She liked
feeling in total control. As she again parked in the
driveway of her home, she recalled the surge of heat
that had traveled up her arm when she'd touched him.
It was merely nerves, she reasoned, and pushed it out
of her mind.

"Well?" Kate demanded, standing in the kitchen
door with her hands on her hips, watching Meg climb
out of her car and walk toward the house.

"Zeke will be here at two on Sunday for his first
lesson," Meg replied.

Kate nodded approvingly. "Neil called while you were gone." Stepping back from the doorway, she allowed Meg to enter. "Said he'd call back."

The phone started ringing before Kate had finished speaking.

"Just wanted to let you know I'd be picking you up around eight for the dance tonight," Neil said when Meg answered.

"Fine," she replied, patiently waiting for what was to come next.

"I hope you're going to wear your gray wool dress," he added coaxingly.

Meg frowned into the receiver. She had been flattered when Neil had started asking her out. He was considered to be the best catch in town. He was thirty years old, six feet tall, with a medium build, thick brownish-blond hair and handsome features. He was also a full partner in a very prestigious law practice and his family was the most prominent in Vincent's Gap. His paternal ancestors had been among the original settlers. George Talmage, Neil's father, owned a major bank as well as other properties in this small farming community just south of Kansas City, Missouri. It was also rumored that he owned shares in banks in St. Louis and Kansas City. Ruth Talmage, Neil's mother, was from the upper social circle in Kansas City and Neil was used to mingling with the moneyed class.

Meg had not minded when he discreetly suggested that she needed to improve her wardrobe. He had, after all, spent a great deal of time among the chic of society. She had refused to permit him to purchase clothing for her, but she had allowed him to go along with her when she went into Kansas City on a shopping spree.

And she hadn't regretted it. He had excellent taste. It had been a bit of a strain on her wallet, but she'd always lived frugally and decided she deserved a little extravagance. However, Neil's habit of "suggesting" what she should wear whenever they were going someplace was getting on her nerves. She was about to say something to him, but she'd had enough confrontations for one day. Besides, she'd been planning to wear the gray dress, anyway. "Of course, I'll wear the gray dress," she replied.

"Good." His voice was filled with triumphant relief.

The Fall Harvest Dance was a big social occasion in Vincent's Gap and obviously Neil wanted to be certain she lived up to Talmage standards, Meg thought sarcastically. Frowning at the phone she was tempted to claim a headache and refuse to attend. *You're overreacting,* she admonished herself. You've had a difficult day and it isn't fair to take it out on Neil. "See you at eight," she repeated the time and after a friendly goodbye, hung up.

"Your voice sounds cheerful, but you don't look happy," Kate observed, studying her daughter. "If you don't like Neil telling you what to wear, you should tell him so."

Meg shrugged. "He means well," she said in his defense. "I'm fairly certain he wants to marry me and because of that he wants me to fit in with his family and their social circle. You can't blame him for that."

"And you can't live your life as a puppet with someone else pulling the strings," Kate countered.

"I'm not a puppet. I prefer to think of myself as his student," Meg rebutted. Then having had all the confrontations she could stand for the moment, she added tightly, "I have a monstrous headache. I'm going to go soak in the hot tub for a while."

Later in the privacy of her bath, Meg carried on a debate that had been running through her mind for the past few weeks. If Neil did ask her to marry him, should she say yes or should she say no? She was realistic enough to know that at twenty-seven she was on her way to spinsterhood if she didn't marry Neil. And he was a wonderful catch.

I should be ecstatic that he's taken an interest in me, she told herself. The problem was she didn't feel ecstatic. *It's been a long day and I'm too tired to feel ecstatic about anything,* she reasoned curtly, pulling the plug and letting the water drain out of the tub.

Her nerves were still on edge when she went back downstairs. Seeing the set of her mother's jaw, she groaned mentally. She knew that look. It meant that Kate did not consider their previous conversation finished.

"I think it's time we had a mother-daughter talk," Kate announced as she and Meg seated themselves at the dinner table.

"It's been a long day," Meg replied, adding with a plea, "Couldn't this wait?"

Kate shook her head. "I may have waited too long as it is." Studying her daughter narrowly, she said, "Are you in love with Neil Talmage?"

Meg had never been good at lying to her mother. Besides, she wasn't certain of the answer. "I like Neil and we get along very well."

"I didn't ask if you liked him," Kate persisted. "I asked if you love him."

Meg stared at the food on her plate. "I don't know," she confessed.

"But you are considering marrying him if he should ask?" Kate continued, her intonation making this statement a question.

Meg's jaw hardened defensively. "I want a husband and children before I'm too old to have them. Neil's a good man. He would make a wonderful father and he would treat me well."

Kate shook her head. "I blame myself for this. When you graduated from college I should never have let you come back here and burden yourself with me. But your father had just died in that car accident and having you here was such a comfort, even though I knew it was selfish." Regret mingled with frustration in Kate's voice. "I limited your opportunities and now you feel forced to marry a man you don't love, just so you can have a family of your own."

"You have never been a burden," Meg assured her mother honestly. "I like living here in Vincent's Gap. I enjoy my job, even though I admit that I complain sometimes, and I like being with you. And," she added with firm confidence, "if I do decide to marry

Neil, it will certainly not be a sacrifice. He is very good husband material and I will make him a good wife.''

Kate studied her daughter with concern. "Sounds to me as if you're trying a bit too hard to convince yourself of that.''

Meg regarded her mother dryly. "Considering the divorce rate in this country, maybe basing a marriage on practical reasons rather than some irrational passion is the best route.''

Leaving her chair, Kate came around the table and gave her daughter a hug. "You've always been a practical child, but if you want my opinion, you need love in a marriage to get through those rough times. And I don't know of a marriage that hasn't had some.''

Although Meg was almost totally convinced her reasoning was sound, a nagging doubt remained at the back of her mind. "I'll think about what you've said,'' she promised, returning her mother's hug.

Neil arrived full of apologies. "I wanted to spend this evening alone with you,'' he said with an impatient frown. "But the Marlows came for a visit and Mother insisted that Sally should come to the dance with us.''

Meg knew that Mrs. Marlow and Mrs. Talmage were as close as sisters. They had grown up together in the same social circle in Kansas City and had been roommates at boarding school. Through the years the two women had remained steadfast friends even though Brenda Marlow now lived in Houston, Texas.

This friendship had also extended to their children. Meg had met Sally Marlow before and liked her. Sally was a pretty girl with platinum-blond hair and blue eyes just a shade lighter in color than Neil's. She was seven years younger than Neil and he talked about her and treated her as if she was his kid sister. "I really don't mind," Meg told him honestly. His manner suggested he had been thinking about proposing tonight, and she wasn't ready with an answer just yet.

"I am so sorry," Sally apologized, as Meg climbed into the car. "I know you and Neil don't need a third wheel, but Mom and Mrs. Talmage refused to listen."

"It's really all right," Meg assured her.

Still Sally looked uncomfortable as she settled into the backseat.

The dance was at the VFW hall, and when they arrived the parking lot was already almost overflowing.

Meg spotted Zeke Wilson's truck and frowned. She was in no mood to face that man again today. Then reminding herself that she had attended numerous social functions where he too had been and that their paths had never crossed, she pushed the thought of him to the back of her mind and continued inside. But the moment she was in the hall, she found herself looking around to see where Zeke was. Spotting him on the dance floor with Rita, she scowled at herself for seeking him out and jerked her gaze away.

"There's a table in the far corner," Neil said, taking each of the women by the arm and guiding them across the room.

Once they were seated, he left them to go for drinks. When he returned, there was a mischievous gleam in his eyes. "Could be an interesting night," he said, seating himself between Sally and Meg. "I just saw Frank Gaint, Rita's ex-husband. He's drunk and talking about reclaiming his wife from Zeke Wilson."

Against her will, Meg's gaze traveled around the room until it fell on Zeke and his pretty redheaded partner near the far side of the dance floor. Out of the corner of her eye she saw Frank Gaint watching them. Then suddenly Frank turned and stalked out of the hall. "Looks like Frank changed his mind," she said.

"Facing Zeke Wilson is something no man takes lightly," Neil observed. "I heard he once bent a crowbar with his bare hands to win a bet."

Meg had heard the same story and she didn't doubt it. Vividly she recalled the strength she had felt when her hand had caught Zeke's arm.

"He sounds dangerous," Sally observed, squinting her eyes for a better look.

He is, Meg thought, then scowled at herself. She was overreacting again. "Zeke doesn't go looking for trouble." Her jaw tensed. She had defended him. *I simply spoke the truth,* she rationalized coolly. *I've never been a person to let unfounded rumors circulate about anyone, even someone as bullheaded as Zeke Wilson.*

"He might not go looking for it, but it looks like he's found it tonight," Neil remarked.

Turning in the direction Neil was looking, Meg saw that Frank had returned. He seemed a little more unsteady than when he'd first left.

"He must have a bottle out in his car he's using to give himself courage," Neil said, voicing aloud what Meg had been thinking.

As Frank started across the dance floor, a couple of his friends tried to stop him but he shook them off. The song the band was playing ended and Meg realized that Zeke and Rita were within a scant few feet of where she, Neil and Sally were sitting. Staggering slightly, Frank reached Zeke and Rita before they could start back to their table.

"I've come to reclaim my wife," Frank announced, meeting Zeke's gaze levelly. Although Frank was a couple of inches shorter and much slighter than Zeke, he was wiry and a real scrapper.

Meg knew that if this turned into a fight both men would get hurt, and she found herself suddenly worried about Zeke. *It's just a humanitarian concern,* she told herself curtly. She'd be concerned about anyone a drunk tried to pick a fight with. Still, her whole body tensed.

"I'm not your wife any longer," Rita interjected angrily before Zeke could respond. "You left me to chase that black-haired hussy from Hannibal."

Frank's gaze shifted to his wife. "I was wrong. I love you, Rita. I want you back and I'm willing to fight for you." His attention shifted back to Zeke. "You and me are going to step outside."

Zeke scowled impatiently. "You're drunk. You need to go home and sleep it off."

"If you won't step outside, I'll nail you right where you stand," Frank growled. His fist shot out at Zeke's chin.

But before it made contact, Zeke caught him by the wrist. "There'll be no brawling in here or we'll both get kicked out, and I don't like being kicked out of any place," Zeke said grimly. In a tone that left no doubt this was an order he expected to be obeyed, Zeke finished in cold, clipped tones, "Now I'm going to let go of you and you're going to walk peacefully out the door."

"You coming with me, or are you too cowardly to fight?" Frank demanded with a sneer.

Meg saw Zeke's eyes narrow dangerously and Frank paled. "I'm coming," Zeke replied with barely controlled patience.

"He didn't mean that, Zeke," Rita spoke up quickly, looking anxiously from one man to the other. "He's real drunk." Her voice took on a plea. "Maybe I'd better take him home. He's too drunk to drive himself, and while he doesn't deserve it, I still feel responsible for him."

"First I'm going to fight for you," Frank insisted.

Zeke and Rita followed, as Frank turned and staggered toward the door.

"You can't fight him," Meg heard Rita saying to Zeke as they moved away. "He's in no condition to defend himself."

"I won't hurt him," Zeke promised.

Meg saw the concern on Rita's face. Realizing it was for Frank, she felt a sharp jab of anger toward the woman. Zeke wouldn't be stepping out to fight a drunk if it wasn't for the redhead, and Rita was worried about the drunk.

Half the people in the hall followed the trio outside. Meg, who had never concerned herself with such things before, had to fight the desire to go with them.

"Aren't you interested in what's going to happen?" Sally demanded excitedly, when Neil and Meg remained seated.

"We'll get a blow-by-blow description," Neil assured her.

Immediately he was proven right. "What's going on out there?" another of the attendees who had remained seated demanded of the crowd that stood in the doorway.

"Nothing," came a disgusted reply. "Frank keeps taking swings at Zeke. Zeke keeps stepping out of the way and Frank keeps falling."

"Rita's stepped in and she's giving Frank a piece of her mind now," another took up the narrative.

"She's making him give her his car keys," a woman spoke up. "Right smart of her. In his condition he shouldn't be walking much less driving."

"Looks like Rita is taking Frank home," a male voice said with disappointment.

Those who had left began to file back inside and the band started playing again.

Meg found herself feeling relieved that Zeke hadn't been hurt. She was also relieved that he would be out of her life for the rest of the evening. As hard as she tried, she was having trouble ignoring him and she needed to concentrate on Neil. She had to sort through her feelings before he proposed.

Suddenly she stiffened. Zeke hadn't left. He'd come back into the hall and he was heading in her direction.

"Evening, Neil, Miss Delany," Zeke said as he came to a halt at their table. His attention focused on Sally, and he smiled charmingly as he said in an easy drawl, "I don't believe we've met."

"Sally, this is Ezekiel Wilson. Zeke, this is Sally Marlow," Neil performed the introductions with a cold politeness that left no doubt he was displeased by Zeke's show of interest in Sally.

Meg forced an indifferent smile as her stomach suddenly twisted uncomfortably at the sight of the big farmer paying attention to the blonde. It felt like jealousy, but that was absurd. She had no personal interest in Zeke Wilson.

Ignoring the dismissal in Neil's voice that had accompanied the introduction, Zeke continued to smile down at Sally. "Evening, Miss Marlow." Then turning his attention back to Neil, he said, "Seems I've lost my date, but you have an abundance of beautiful women. Mind if I borrow Miss Marlow for a dance?"

Sally looked to Neil with a plea for help in her eyes. Obviously Zeke frightened her.

"I was just getting ready to take Sally for a turn around the floor myself," Neil replied, rising and holding out his hand toward her.

Meg expected Zeke to leave as Neil and Sally moved out onto the dance floor, but instead she found herself under the full brunt of his dark gaze. "Guess that leaves you and me, Miss Delany," he said, extending his hand toward her.

Feeling like the leftover no one wanted, her mouth formed a firm line. "I really don't..."

"After the way you faced me down this afternoon, I can't believe you're suddenly afraid of me, too." There was a challenge in his voice and cynical laughter in his eyes, as if he found Sally's flight amusing.

"I'm most certainly *not* afraid of you," she returned curtly. Rising, she walked with him to the dance floor.

She saw Neil toss her a "what in the world are you doing?" glare and shrugged her shoulders as if to say she'd had no choice. He rewarded her with a disgruntled glance. This day had gone from bad to worse and beyond, she mused. Then suddenly she was in Zeke's arms moving to the slow rhythm of a country-and-western song. As his hand pressed gently against her back, an excitement stirred deep within her. Curtly she told herself she was just overly tense. But that explanation didn't help. A heat ignited by the contact of his large calloused hand holding hers was beginning to travel along her arm. She drew a deep breath in her effort to regain control of her senses. It didn't work. Instead she was acutely aware of the very masculine scent of his after-shave. The high-heeled shoes she was wearing gave added height to her five-foot-five inch frame, putting her on easy eye level with his neck. He was holding her loosely and she had the most tremendous urge to move closer and rest her forehead against his strong jawline. *This is crazy!* she berated herself.

Desperate to take her mind off her body's intense reaction to Zeke's touch, she said, "I'm sorry about Rita."

He smiled lazily. "I told you this afternoon, she and I are only friends. I gave her a little comfort when she needed it, but she's in love with Frank."

Meg's teeth fastened on the inside of her bottom lip as she suddenly found herself wondering what it would feel like to have Zeke comfort her. *Stop this!* she ordered herself. Other than on a professional level, she and Zeke Wilson didn't belong in each other's lives.

But when the dance ended and he led her back to her table, she couldn't deny the tight little knot in her stomach as she wondered if once again he was going to ask Sally to dance. *I'm not jealous, I simply don't want any trouble,* she told herself seeing the frown on Neil's face.

To her relief Zeke didn't ask Sally for the next dance. Instead he simply thanked Meg, said his good-byes to Neil and Sally and wandered off to the far side of the room.

"He's very rough-looking," Sally remarked in a hushed whisper, as if she was afraid Zeke might hear her.

"He's always been a law-abiding citizen," Meg heard herself replying sharply. She'd come to Zeke's defense again! When Sally's eyes widened in surprise,

Meg added in a more moderate tone, "But he does have a very overbearing way about him."

The band was playing another slow dance and Neil rose and held his hand out toward Meg. She knew from the grim look on his face that he had something he wanted to say to her and he didn't want Sally to hear. Rising, she allowed him to lead her out onto the dance floor.

"I cannot understand why you danced with the man," he said angrily as he took her in his arms and they began to move to the music.

"Because I couldn't think of a polite excuse not to," she replied. Anxiously she waited for the heat of his hand to move along her arm. But nothing happened . . . not even a lukewarm tingle . . . nothing.

"A simple 'no' should have sufficed," he replied testily.

"Well it didn't." Feeling unfairly chastised, she added tersely, "And I don't know why you're so angry with me. You were the one who went off and left me alone with him."

"I knew Sally didn't know how to handle the man. She's just a kid," he responded in his defense. In a semblance of apology, he added in a slightly teasing tone, "You're a teacher. You're supposed to know how to handle unruly males."

It occurred to Meg that no one would ever "handle" Zeke Wilson. But she kept this thought to herself. Still shaken by the unnerving sensations she'd experienced in Zeke's arms, she willed her body to react to Neil as she leaned closer, resting her head against his jaw. He felt comfortable, but there was no excitement. Comfortable is a good quality, she told herself.

Taking her movement toward him as a sign of forgiveness and affection, Neil smiled and tightened his hold on her. "Next time I'll take both of you and hold one in each arm," he promised in her ear.

His breath stirred the hairs on the back of her neck. It tickled, but nothing more.

Zeke left about half an hour later. She was angry with herself for even caring about his comings and goings, still she was glad he was gone.

But his absence didn't help her jumbled nerves. As the dance continued, a monumental headache began to build at her temples. "I hate to cut short the evening, but I really think you should take me home," she finally said to Neil as the throbbing grew worse.

Sally frowned solicitously as the trio walked to Neil's car. "I hope you're not coming down with the flu."

"I'm sure it's just a headache," Meg replied. All she wanted was to escape to the solitude of her room. She felt like a bundle of disorienting emotions. Suddenly afraid that Neil might be thinking of dropping Sally off first so that he could have some private time with her, Meg added, "But I do think I should go directly home."

A little later as Neil stood with her on the front porch of her house, he confirmed her fear as he said regretfully, "I really wanted some time alone with you this evening."

"There'll be other evenings," she replied, adding to herself, *ones when I'll be thinking more clearly.*

The regret in his voice grew stronger. "I have to fly to Houston tomorrow. Mrs. Marlow has a delicate legal matter she wants me to handle personally, so I'm accompanying her and Sally when they return home. From the way she has described the situation I probably won't be back until next Friday." He smiled with self-assurance. "Keep it open for me." Then taking her loosely in his arms he kissed her lightly, instead of the long, passionate kiss she had expected. "Don't want to give the kid any ideas," he said with an edge of self-consciousness, nodding slightly toward the car as he released her.

Meg was tempted to point out that Sally was not a kid. She was twenty-three and filled out her dress nicely. But the thought brought Zeke Wilson sharply back into her mind. The image of him smiling down at Sally caused the pounding in her head to increase and giving Neil a final light kiss, she slipped inside.

"Have a nice time?" Kate asked, coming out of the living room where she'd been watching television.

"Yes," Meg answered absently. Then she shook her head. "Truth is I had a rotten time."

Kate looked apologetic. "I hope I didn't spoil your evening. I just felt we needed to have that little talk."

"You didn't spoil my evening," Meg assured her. Again Zeke Wilson's image came into her mind. "I've just got this splitting headache," she said, and started up the stairs.

"Take a couple of aspirin and go to bed," Kate recommended. "You look exhausted."

Meg nodded.

A little later as she lay snuggled beneath her heavy comforter, she told herself it had just been an unusually weird day. The unnerving reactions she was having to Zeke Wilson were due to an ion imbalance in the atmosphere. "Or maybe those wayward spirits of ghosts and goblins that are supposed to come out on Halloween are getting an early start," she muttered. Then her jaw tightening with determination, she thought with assurance, *tomorrow I'll be back to my old self.*

Chapter Three

The next morning dawned bright and clear. There was a slight briskness in the air, but the temperature was mild for October. Right after breakfast Meg called Mrs. Royd and arranged to go by and see her around ten. Norma Royd had been her first-grade teacher, and her father's and her mother's first-grade teacher. Although the woman was nearly eighty now, her mind was still sharp and she was known for her discretion. If anyone could help Meg set up a proper learning program for Zeke, it was Norma Royd.

At ten sharp, Meg knocked on Norma's door.

"I am curious about what brings you to my doorstep," the elderly teacher said, greeting Meg with a smile and ushering her into the living room.

On the coffee table was a pot of tea, two cups and a plate full of homemade cookies. Seating herself on the couch, Meg wetted her suddenly dry lips. Mrs. Royd was an astute woman and while Meg was seeking her help, she didn't want to say anything to give away Zeke's identity.

"You always used to do that when you were nervous," Mrs. Royd observed with a knowing look, as she seated herself in a chair opposite Meg. "What is bothering you, dear?"

A mildly embarrassed flush reddened Meg's cheeks. "I need your promise you won't tell anyone what I'm about to tell you," she requested, hoping the woman wouldn't be offended.

"You have my word," Mrs. Royd assured her, showing no evidence she had taken offense. "Now have a cup of tea and tell me what is on your mind."

Accepting the tea, Meg took a sip. Then without using Zeke's name, she explained his request. "I was wondering if you had any books I could use or if you could suggest some," she finished.

Norma Royd smiled brightly. "I've just the thing. Fact is, I've been tutoring a few adults myself. Now that's a secret you can keep for me." Rising, she added, "You finish your tea and I'll go get the books."

Breathing a sigh of relief that at least this one problem was solved, Meg took another sip of the tea and nibbled on a cookie.

"Now that he's made the decision to learn to read, I know Zeke will prove to be an excellent student,"

Mrs. Royd said as she returned and handed Meg the books.

Meg's eyes rounded in surprise. She could have sworn she had said nothing to give away the identity of her student. "How in the world did you guess?"

"Simple deduction mixed with a bit of gossip," the woman replied with a smile. "Lucile saw Zeke's truck at your house yesterday and has been speculating ever since, with whomever will listen, as to why he was there."

Meg frowned. Lucile Tate lived across the street from her mother's house and was a vigilant observer and an even more ardent gossip. "Lucile Tate could prove to be a real problem," she muttered.

"Most definitely, along with all the other nosey parkers in this town," Mrs. Royd agreed, seating herself and pouring another cup of tea. "Since I'm certain Zeke wants to learn as quickly as possible, that will mean frequent lessons. Whether you two meet at your home, his farm or out in the wild, people will eventually find out you're seeing one another. It is very difficult for anything to remain an absolute secret in this town for long. Of course you could keep the reading lessons confidential by letting people think the two of you were seeing one another romantically." Mrs. Royd frowned and shook her head. "But that would cause trouble between you and Neil." Her frown instantly became a smile, and her voice took on a motherly prying quality as she continued without a pause, "I understand the two of you have been seeing each other very regularly. There is even talk of a possible wedding."

"I have been seeing Neil," Meg confirmed noncommittally. She'd been so concerned about getting the materials together to begin Zeke's lessons, she hadn't thought about Zeke's suggestion or the need to provide some reason to be meeting with him so often. The truth was, she mused, ever since Zeke's unexpected intrusion into her life she hadn't been thinking totally clearly, at all. But Zeke's idea of linking him to her romantically was definitely out of the question. Neil would be furious. Besides, what if Neil did ask her to marry him and she said yes? If they were using the pretense that Zeke was interested in her romantically, he would have to stop seeing her. "And you're right, letting people think Zeke was courting me would cause a great many problems."

"Then we must come up with a plan." Mrs. Royd's eyes sparkled with excitement.

"But what?" The image of the farmer smiling down at Sally Marlow came sharply into her mind and the recollection of being second choice washed over her. Meg frowned in agitation. She wasn't interested in being any choice of Zeke Wilson's. Aloud she said, "I can't think of a single reason Zeke Wilson and I should spend any time together." Mrs. Royd glanced toward her with a questioning frown and Meg realized she had sounded much too vehement. "Our paths have never crossed before, and as far as I know we have no interests in common," she added in milder tones.

"I have an idea," Norma Royd said hesitantly. "It's a bit wicked."

Meg studied the elderly teacher narrowly. She'd never thought Mrs. Royd had a devilish bone in her body. "Wicked?"

Mrs. Royd pursed her mouth thoughtfully. "Well, more of a prank than truly wicked. After all this is the season for tricks."

"True," Meg agreed, smiling at the mischievous sparkle in Mrs. Royd's eyes. "What is your idea?"

"Well, your mother and father used to play a marvelous game of bridge. But Kate hasn't played since Joe died. So for the past five years Lucile and Tom have won every tournament. I wouldn't mind that so much, except that Lucile has developed quite an ego where her bridge-playing is involved. If she's sitting at your table and you make a mistake, once the hand is completed you have to listen to her play-by-play description of how you should have bid and played it. She can get on a person's nerves." Mrs. Royd shook her head, then used her fingers to comb back a strand of white hair that had escaped from the bun at the nape of her neck. "Anyway, we could throw everyone off by completely avoiding linking your name with Zeke's. Instead we could say that your mother is teaching him how to play bridge so the two of them can enter the spring tournament. It'll give Lucile something to fret about, so she'll leave the rest of us alone for a while."

"I suppose when I'm finished tutoring Zeke, we could say he decided he didn't have the time to compete. That would be around planting time and he would be busy," Meg mused. Playing a harmless trick on Mrs. Tate did appeal to her inner sense of justice. All her life, Lucile Tate had spied on her. If she did anything a little on the naughty side, it was around town in an instant. Her teenage years had been the worst. If she got home late from a date, the whole town knew by noon the next day. And Lucile Tate wasn't above embellishing the details of any story she told.

"Then it's settled. As soon as you're gone, I'll phone Lucile." Norma Royd smiled mischievously. "She'll have it all over town by the end of the day."

"Then I'd better warn my mother and Zeke," Meg said, setting her cup aside.

Reaching across the table, Mrs. Royd took Meg's hand in hers. "I'm so glad you're going to help Zeke. He was one of my most regrettable failures. But it wasn't his fault. He was a bright boy." Releasing Meg, she sighed deeply. "He just got so far behind, he stopped trying."

Driving home, Meg again found herself picturing Zeke as a lost and lonely little boy. Then the image of the man impinged. There was nothing lost or lonely about him. The memory of his embrace as he guided her around the dance floor came back sharply. In spite of the chill in the air, a sudden rush of warmth spread over her. "No," she snapped. She refused to feel any interest in a man like Zeke Wilson. He was bullheaded and stubborn and he preferred blondes and redheads. She scowled at herself for caring what he preferred. *I'm just overwrought,* she assured herself. This whole business had set her nerves on edge.

Turning onto Maple Street, Meg suddenly stiffened. Lucile Tate was leaving her mother's house. It had been no more than three minutes since Meg had left Mrs. Royd. Lucile couldn't have heard the bridge story yet. Meg just hoped her mother hadn't invented something else. Too many stories floating around was going to make the whole situation seem very suspicious. "I should have told Mrs. Royd to wait until I'd talked to my mother and Zeke," she muttered, angry with herself for not thinking of this sooner. She was definitely not her usual practical self today.

Entering the house a couple of minutes later, she found her mother in the kitchen.

"Lucile came over to pump me about why Zeke was here yesterday," Kate informed Meg with a gleam in her eyes. "Apparently Rita and Frank ran off to Las Vegas to get remarried and Lucile thinks Zeke has turned his attention toward you."

Meg frowned worriedly. That was precisely what she didn't want people to think. "What did you tell her?"

"I didn't tell her a thing." Kate smiled triumphantly. "Every time she mentioned Zeke, I changed the subject."

"Good." Meg breathed a sigh of relief.

"Of course once Lucile gets a bee in her bonnet, she's determined to have her say. She was full of advice as to how I should strongly discourage you from getting any romantic notions about Zeke. She went through the whole litany of women he's been linked with and how he's always managed to escape before he was roped into a wedding," Kate continued in an amused tone. Then her expression became serious. "To be real honest, I like Zeke, and if he didn't seem to have such an aversion to marriage I'd encourage you to flirt with him."

Meg frowned reprovingly. "Don't be ridiculous."

Kate's mouth formed a pout. "I just don't like you feeling that you don't have a choice when it comes to husbands."

Meg's frown deepened. Her nerves were too on edge for another confrontation with her mother. "I really don't want to discuss my marital situation at the moment," she said firmly. "Besides, I have a more immediate problem to talk to you about. Mrs. Royd and I came up with a story to tell people about why Zeke is coming over."

Kate frowned reprovingly. "I thought you promised Zeke you wouldn't tell anyone that he was the one coming for lessons."

"I didn't tell her," Meg replied defensively. "She guessed. Lucile has already spread it all over town that Zeke was here yesterday."

Kate shook her head. "I do wish Lucile would find something better to do with her time." Her attention returned to Meg. "What story did you come up with?"

"We'll tell people that he's coming over the learn to play bridge with you, so the two of you can enter the spring tournament," Meg explained, hoping her mother wouldn't object.

"I haven't played bridge since Joe died," Kate murmured, a shadow of sadness clouding her eyes. "But then Zeke and I really wouldn't be playing anyway." The shadow faded and amusement entered her eyes. "That would stir things up around here, wouldn't it?"

"Maybe a little," Meg confirmed.

"Better tell Zeke before the grapevine gets to him," Kate cautioned.

Nodding, Meg pulled out the phone book and looked up Zeke's number. She dialed but got no answer.

"It's a nice day for a drive. It feels more like spring than fall. This could be our last reasonably comfortable day before winter hits," Kate said as Meg hung up. "Why don't we go on out there? He's probably in the barn or some such place. We really need to tell him before he talks to anyone. The story is going to be all over town by this afternoon."

Meg had a tremendous desire to refuse. The thought of seeing Zeke made her uneasy. *You're being ridiculous,* she chided herself. *You're going to be seeing the man every day for the next few months.* "I suppose you're right," she conceded.

It was hard to believe, she thought a few minutes later as she and Kate headed west out of town, *that yesterday morning Zeke Wilson had no place in her life and now it seemed to be revolving around him. But only temporarily and only on an impersonal basis,* she stipulated.

"It's been nearly five years since Pete Wilson passed away now," Kate said as Meg parked in front of the two-story farmhouse. "Big place for a man alone. Must get right lonely here for Zeke."

"It's his choice," Meg pointed out as she climbed from the car and waited for her mother to join her.

Kate smiled knowingly. "One of these days the right woman will come along and knock him off his feet."

Meg again found herself remembering the feel of Zeke's hands holding her as they danced. Curtly she reminded herself that she'd been his second choice. If someone was going to knock Zeke Wilson off his feet, it wasn't her. The thought caused an unexpected, sharp twist in her stomach. "Zeke Wilson's private life is not our concern," she said tersely.

Kate glanced toward her daughter. "I was only making conversation. You certainly are on edge today."

"I'm not very good at subterfuge," Meg replied, not wanting her mother to guess that it was Zeke Wilson who was making her so edgy. She didn't like admitting it to herself.

"Well, it's just a little white lie and it's for a very good cause," Kate reasoned.

Meg rewarded this observation with a shrug. "His truck is here," she said over her shoulder, walking rapidly toward the house. All she wanted was to get this visit over with and leave. "He should be here somewhere."

There was no answer to her knock on the door. Almost with relief she turned back to her mother.

"There's no telling where he might be. This farm covers a lot of acreage. We'll have to call him later."

"No, we won't." Kate raised her hand and waved widely. Following the direction of her mother's gaze, Meg saw Zeke approaching from the direction of the barn.

"Morning, ladies," he said as he reached them. Glancing at his watch, he corrected himself. "Afternoon."

"Afternoon," Meg heard herself saying, as she found herself watching a thin stream of perspiration making its way from beneath the brim of his Stetson and moving slowly down to his jawline. He smelled of hay and his clothes were streaked with dirt. Taking off his hat, he wiped at the rivulet of sweat with the sleeve of his heavy flannel shirt. Then, replacing his hat on his head, he pulled off the heavy leather work gloves he'd been wearing. In spite of her best effort not to, Meg once again found herself vividly recalling the feel of those strong, calloused hands as they had held her. *Stop it,* she ordered herself.

"And to what do I owe the pleasure of this visit," Zeke asked with an easy smile.

"We wanted to warn you," Kate said before Meg could speak.

Zeke's smile was replaced with a frown as his gaze narrowed accusingly on Meg. "Warn me?"

It was obvious he thought she had blurted out his secret to the world. Her jaw tightened with self-righteous indignation. "Only Norma Royd and my mother know the real reason you are coming to see me. Mrs. Royd knows because she guessed when I went to her for materials. It was already all over town that you had been to my home. But you don't have to worry, she will keep your secret. My mother knows..." Meg caught herself before she admitted that Kate had eavesdropped, and said instead, "...because I don't like lying to her. Besides she had to be told the truth. We will be conducting your lessons in our home. She was bound to notice and I needed her help in providing a story to explain your frequent visits to the house." Frostily she added, "For my own personal reasons I felt it was best not to let people link us romantically."

"Suit yourself," he said with an indifferent shrug. "What do you have in mind?"

Concisely Meg explained the ploy Norma Royd had devised.

"Sounds fine to me," Zeke said when she finished.

"If you're free this evening you could come over for some dinner and afterward I'll teach you a few terms and a little about the game, so you'll sound knowledgeable," Kate suggested.

Outwardly Meg maintained a polite facade. Inwardly she balked. She wanted to keep her contact with Zeke on a strictly professional basis and her mother was inviting him over for a social evening. *Of course it's not really social,* she reasoned. *It's simply to aid the ploy. Besides he probably won't come.*

But before this last thought was even complete, Zeke smiled and raising his hat toward Kate he said in an easy drawl, "I've heard that your cooking is the best in the county. I'd be a fool to pass up such an invitation."

Kate blushed with pleasure. "Come around about six-thirty, then."

"You can count on it," Zeke replied.

"That man has a right charming way about him," Kate said as Meg drove them back to town. The older woman's cheeks were still flushed with pleasure.

It occurred to Meg that Zeke had displayed his charm with every woman she'd seen him with except for her. It was as if he didn't even view her as a woman. She felt insulted. "Some people find rattlesnakes charming," she heard herself saying.

"Margaret Delany!" Kate reprimanded. "I don't understand why you've taken such a dislike to the man."

"I don't dislike him," Meg replied stiffly, wishing that she did. It would be a lot easier to deal with than the disturbing emotions he was causing to stir within her.

Kate frowned at her. "Well, you sure could've fooled me."

"He's just placed me in a difficult situation," Meg elaborated in her defense.

"The man is simply asking you to do what you've been trained to do, teach," Kate countered, the reprimand still in her voice.

"I know," Meg conceded. The problem wasn't Zeke. It was her. These reactions she was having to him were unnerving. As much as she hated admitting it, she was attracted to him. But he definitely wasn't the man of her dreams. She was the marrying kind and obviously he wasn't. Besides, even if he was the marrying kind, he wasn't interested in her.

The phone was ringing when they arrived back at the house. It was Neil calling to tell Meg that he and the Marlows had arrived safely. "We're going out to dinner and then the opera," he informed her, adding, "sure wish you were here."

"I wish I was, too," she replied and it wasn't a lie. She wasn't interested in a night at the opera, but she was dreading spending the evening with Zeke Wilson.

As she hung up, she glared at herself in the mirror. *You're behaving like a schoolgirl,* she chided herself. *Besides, I won't be spending the evening with him. He'll be in the living room with Mom and I'll be in my bedroom going over the books Mrs. Royd loaned me. I won't even know he's here.*

But that evening she again learned that Zeke Wilson wasn't an easy man to ignore. He arrived with a bouquet of flowers that brought an exclamation of delight from her mother. Meg thanked him, too, but never let herself forget for one moment that the blooms were really for Kate.

"You'd best save room for dessert," Kate admonished him as they sat down at the dinner table. "Meg made an apple pie and it smells wonderful."

Zeke smiled dryly. "Guess I'd better take advantage of that. Once she's married to a Talmage, she won't be doing any more baking. She'll have servants to see to her every need.''

The hint of mockery in his voice caused Meg's back to stiffen. ''If I marry Neil, it won't be because he can provide me with servants.''

''I didn't mean any offense,'' Zeke apologized stiffly.

Meg felt a flush creeping up her neck and wished she'd kept her retort to herself. Other people had teased her about the easy life she'd have if she married Neil, and it hadn't bothered her. *You've got to stop overreacting to Zeke Wilson,* she reprimanded herself.

Kate tossed Meg an ''I don't understand what's gotten into you'' glance, then guided the conversation to farming.

''The drought hit pretty hard this year,'' Zeke admitted with a grim expression. ''But I was able to put away enough feed for my cattle and hogs to last the winter.''

Meg had always heard that Zeke was a good farmer; that he knew how to work the land to get the most value from it. Of course, that also meant long, hard hours of labor. Momentarily she found herself recalling how he'd looked with the sweat running down his jaw and the smell of straw coming from his clothes. Again an excitement stirred within her. *Stop it!* she ordered herself. These feelings were totally irrational. Still she couldn't help wishing that Neil made her feel this way.

Finally the meal was over. Desperately in need of time alone to get rid of these disturbing reactions she was having toward Zeke Wilson, Meg insisted that he and her mother go into the living room and start his bridge lessons while she did the dishes. But as she put her first load of plates down and started back toward the dining room, she nearly collided with Zeke.

"Wouldn't be fair for you to have to do all the carrying and the washing," he said, his hold tightening securely on the serving platter he was carrying.

His arm brushed against Meg as he continued into the kitchen and currents of heat rushed through her. *This is really crazy,* she chided herself. Determined to get rid of him as quickly as possible, she moved swiftly toward the table.

Kate joined in, too, and within only a few minutes all of the dishes and leftovers were in the kitchen. "Now you two run along," Meg ordered firmly. This time they obeyed.

Alone at last, she drew a deep breath of relief. To her chagrin the fading scent of Zeke's after-shave tantalized her senses. "This has got to stop!" she ordered herself in a harsh whisper. Zeke Wilson barely noticed she was a female, and even if he did become more aware of her, he wasn't the marrying kind. Whereas, Neil was definitely attracted to her and he was the marrying kind. So what if he did feel she needed a bit of polishing to fit into his social circle? He was willing to teach her.

After finishing the dishes, Meg started up to her room. But as she passed the living room, Kate waved her in. "Zeke has a wonderful card sense," she announced excitedly. "Must be those weekly poker games I keep hearing rumors about."

Zeke just smiled but said nothing. Gambling was still illegal in the state, except for playing bingo and the state-run lottery.

"Anyway," Kate continued. "He needs to practice a bit of bidding. So I thought you could bid as his partner and I'll bid the other two hands and keep an eye on Zeke's responses."

Meg had no desire to enter into this, but she couldn't think of a polite excuse not to. Forcing a smile, she sat down.

Zeke's long legs were stretched out under the small card table and, as Meg moved her chair in and shifted into a comfortable position, the toes of her shoes touched the toes of the cowboy boots he wore. Immediately tantalizing currents raced up her legs. Jerking her feet back, she positioned them beneath her chair.

"Sorry for taking up so much room," he apologized gruffly, shifting and drawing his feet in closer to his side of the table.

"It's not a problem," she replied coolly. Inwardly she was furious with herself. These reactions to this man had to stop!

For the next hour she forced herself to concentrate on the cards and the bidding. Finally Zeke announced that he felt he had a good enough grasp of the game to talk about it as if he knew what he was doing. Then after again thanking them for dinner, he left.

"He is right pleasant to have around," Kate observed, watching from the front window as Zeke drove away.

"Just don't get too used to having him here," Meg cautioned dryly. For her part, she was determined to get her tutoring over as quickly as possible and get the man out of her life once again.

Chapter Four

"I just couldn't believe it when I heard it," Vera Myers said, crossing the wide front lawn in front of the church to accost Kate and Meg before they could enter the sanctuary Sunday morning. Vera was around Kate's age and was one of the longtime regulars in the bridge club. "Zeke Wilson is actually going to play bridge as your partner." Vera shook her head to add emphasis to her bewilderment. "This will certainly liven up our little group."

Kate smiled. Lowering her voice in a conspiratorial manner, she leaned close to Vera. "I just hope he doesn't decide spending an evening with us older ladies is too boring."

"Don't worry about that," Vera replied in the same lowered, conspiratorial tones. "I hear several of the younger women have suddenly begun to express an interest in joining our little group. We could have a real surge in enrollment. We might even have to go back to having newcomer classes.''

Meg felt a nudging in her stomach. *I am not jealous of the women who chase after Zeke Wilson,* she told herself firmly. They were only asking for trouble, and she was too smart for that. A prickling on the back of her neck caused her to look over her shoulder. Zeke had just arrived and was walking their way.

Vera flushed with pleasure as the dark-eyed farmer smiled and bid her a good morning. Kate's cheeks brightened in color also as he turned his smile to her and wished her a good morning.

He is certainly a roguish charmer, Meg admitted, steeling herself not to react when he turned his charm on her. But she needn't have worried. When his attention shifted to her, although the smile was still on his face, it did not reach his eyes and instead of basking in the warmth of his charm, she found herself chilled by his coolness.

The night before, as she had tossed restless in bed trying to go to sleep, her encounters with him had insisted on playing through her mind and it had occurred to her that his cold, businesslike demeanor toward her could be due to the embarrassment he felt because he'd had to admit to her that he couldn't read. Now it occurred to her that although he had sought out her aid, he simply didn't like her. The thought stung. Feeling the sudden need to escape, she said, ''I promised to help with the nursery today. If you all will excuse me..." Before the others barely had a chance to say goodbye, she was on her way into the church.

Passing down the corridor to the nursery, she caught hostile, envious glances from a couple of the women who flirted with Zeke on Sundays hoping to get noticed. Well they can have him, Meg told herself curtly, forcing a friendly smile for each of them. Entering the nursery, she was accosted by a toddler who wanted to be held. Picking up the child, her smile became genuine as the little girl wrapped her arms around Meg's neck and gave her a hug. A wistful look entered Meg's eyes. This was what she wanted...a family, children of her own and a husband who wanted both her and the children. Again she told herself how lucky she was to have Neil.

By the time church was over, Meg was certain she had the irrational reactions she'd been experiencing toward Zeke well under control. He was a professional obligation she had undertaken. She would think of him in the same way she did any other student.

When her mother announced that he was coming for Sunday dinner, she acknowledged the news with an indifferent shrug.

"And since we walked to church, I accepted a ride home with him," Kate added as Zeke left the group he had been talking with and approached Meg and her mother.

Meg saw the mischievous grin on her mother's face. "You're really enjoying being the center of attention, aren't you?"

"It's been a long time since I stirred up any excitement in this town," Kate replied with a playful laugh.

Meg frowned disgruntledly. "Well, I'm glad one of us is happy about this."

Kate's grin turned into a disapproving pout. "I can remember a time when you would have found all of this very amusing, too...before Neil Talmage stepped into your life and decided to make you over into one of his kind."

"Neil isn't making me over," Meg insisted.

"He tells you what to wear, and I've heard him lecturing you on what to say and what not to say when the two of you are going to one of his mother's swank parties," Kate pointed out.

"And I heard Dad tell you what to say and what not to say on occasion, too," Meg rebutted.

Kate flushed slightly. "Guess you and I do have a way of speaking our minds, and it's not always for the best."

"You two ladies ready to head home?" Zeke asked, joining them abruptly.

Kate glanced at her watch and her eyes widened. "Oh, my, yes. Rev. Howard must have spoken longer today than usual. I just hope my roast isn't burnt."

When they reached the truck, Meg held the door open and waited for her mother to climb in. She had no desire to be sandwiched in the middle of the seat next to Zeke. But Kate held back. "You know I like to be near a window," she said, motioning for Meg to climb in first.

With a mental groan, Meg admitted defeat. Kate had been in the car with her husband when a drunk driver had crashed into them, killing Joe Delany. She had been trapped in the wreckage for nearly two hours before her rescuers had been able to pry her free. That she hadn't been killed was amazing; that she only suffered a couple of broken ribs, one broken arm and a broken leg was a miracle. But the tragedy had left her with a deep-rooted fear, and when she rode in a car she had to be next to a door, with the window open slightly. Bowing to the inevitable, Meg climbed up into the seat and slid toward the middle.

When Zeke climbed in behind the wheel, Meg scooted closer to her mother. Still her shoulder brushed against his several times during the short ride. Each time she was acutely aware of the contact and each time her aggravation with herself grew stronger.

Arriving at the house, Kate waited impatiently while Meg unlocked the front door. Then stripping out of her coat, she tossed it at her daughter. "Make yourself comfortable," she directed Zeke over her shoulder as she rushed toward the kitchen.

"Mind if I take off my suit coat, or do you and your mom like to dress formally for Sunday dinner?" Zeke asked as Meg hung her coat and her mother's in the hall closet.

"You don't need a coat or a tie to eat with us," she replied, waiting for him to hand her the garment. "We're casual people here."

"Going to be a real change for you when you move into a Talmage household," Zeke said as he handed her his coat and tie and unfastened the top button of his shirt.

Meg could have sworn she heard a cynical edge to his voice, but she'd already embarrassed herself once by overreacting to a remark he'd made about Neil and she didn't want to do that a second time. "I'm flexible," she replied with a nonchalant shrug. Finished with hanging up his coat and tie, she nodded toward the living room. "Make yourself comfortable. I'm going to see if my mother can use some help."

But before she could start toward the kitchen, Zeke blocked her way. "There is one thing that has been puzzling me."

His manner was casual, but those dark eyes of his were studying her with an intensity that caused Meg's guard to come to full alert. "And what is that?"

"The other night at the dance, Neil deserted you to protect his young blond friend. That doesn't seem like the action of a man in love. If it had been me, I'd never have left my woman."

That Neil had quickly come to Sally's aid, getting her away from Zeke and leaving Meg to deal with the farmer hadn't bothered Meg. But now that she thought about it, his protective attitude toward Sally did seem unusually strong. Still she wasn't going to admit that to Zeke. "Unlike you, Neil does not have a caveman mentality. He trusts me." Without thinking, she heard herself adding with a hint of sarcasm, "And you frightened Sally."

Amusement sparkled in the dark depths of his eyes. With the tip of his finger, he traced the line of her jaw. "But I don't frighten you, do I, Meg?"

His touch left a trail of fire. "No," she replied stiffly. It was the truth. It was her own reactions to him that unnerved her. Wanting to escape his company, she added tightly, "Now if you will excuse me, I really must go help my mother."

But as she edged around him and started toward the kitchen, he followed. "I've always preferred warm kitchens to cold living rooms," he said in answer to the questioning glance she tossed back at him.

He's like one of those evasive little thorns a person can't get rid of, she mused grudgingly.

"Thought I would offer my services," Zeke said as Kate greeted him with a surprised look. "Everything smells mighty good."

"You can carve the roast while I stir the gravy and Meg sets a third place at the table," Kate directed, accepting his offer without hesitation.

Watching Zeke roll up his shirt sleeves and pick up the knife, Meg was amazed by how natural he looked in this domestic scene. It's strictly an illusion, she told herself curtly. From the gossip she'd heard, he was about as domesticated as an alley cat. Glad to be able to escape for a moment of solitude, she quickly gathered up the place setting and went into the living room.

The phone rang just as she finished putting the utensils in place. Going into the hall she answered it, to discover Neil on the other end of the line.

"Mother just called me," he said, his voice holding a strong note of disapproval. "I don't like the idea of Zeke Wilson hanging around your house."

Meg groaned mentally. Ruth Talmage had wasted no time in notifying her son of the latest development in Vincent's Gap. "He's coming over to learn to play bridge with my mother," she explained calmly. She hated lying to Neil, but she'd made a promise. Besides, it wasn't a total lie. Her mother was teaching Zeke the game.

"I don't care what excuse he's using, I don't like him hanging around you," Neil said curtly.

Meg felt a flush of pleasure. He was jealous. "I can assure you that Zeke Wilson has no interest in me, whatsoever."

"Maybe so," Neil conceded. "You're not his type and I know you're too smart to encourage him. But I don't like all the gossip his hanging around your place is bound to cause."

The flush of pleasure died. He wasn't jealous; he simply didn't like the notoriety Zeke's intrusion into her life had aroused. The Talmages thought of themselves as above reproach and prided themselves on never being the brunt of any unpleasant rumors. Aloud she said coolly, "Everyone in town knows he's coming to see my mother and not me."

"They might know it, but it doesn't make as good a bit of gossip." Skepticism entered Neil's voice. "Besides I find it extremely hard to believe the man is the bridge-playing type."

Meg didn't want an argument. Her nerves were too much on edge. She was likely to say something she might regret. "Well he is," she replied firmly. Then determined to change the subject, she asked, "How is your business progressing?"

"Just fine." His voice continued to hold an edge of impatience. "Hopefully I'll be able to come home sooner than I thought."

There was a promise in his voice that their discussion regarding Zeke Wilson was not finished. Meg breathed a sigh as she hung up a minute later. Obviously it was going to take some work to pacify Neil.

Returning to the dining room, Meg discovered that Kate and Zeke had finished putting all the food on the table. As she joined them and they all sat down, Kate asked, "Who was on the phone?"

"Neil," she replied with schooled nonchalance.

Kate regarded her daughter with concern. "Guess he heard about Zeke."

"He heard," she admitted. Then in a tone that indicated she didn't want to talk about Neil any further, she turned the conversation to a discussion of the sermon they'd just listened to in church.

It wasn't until she and Zeke went into the living room to begin his first lesson that Neil's name was again mentioned.

Meg had set up the card table for them to sit at. But instead of sitting down, Zeke remained standing behind his chair. "I don't want to cause any real trouble between you and Talmage," he said stiffly. "Maybe coming to you wasn't such a good idea."

Meg glared at him. She was tempted to send him on his way. But a stronger part refused to allow her to turn her back on him. "I agreed to teach you to read and you're going to learn," she replied without compromise.

A self-conscious smile tilted one corner of his mouth. "Yes, ma'am," he said, and pulling out his chair, he sat down.

She was worried that when he saw the elementary level at which they would have to start, he might balk. After all, his male pride was sure to be involved. But he didn't. He treated the entire lesson in a businesslike manner, concentrating intently on her instructions.

Meg, however, had a little difficulty with her concentration. The way they were forced to sit in order to share the same text caused her shoulder to brush against his arm periodically and once or twice when one or the other shifted positions, their knees collided slightly. Meg was acutely aware of each contact. Again she found herself wishing that Neil affected her this way. *Neil can offer you a secure home and children,* her practical side pointed out curtly. With firm determination, she ignored the disquieting sensations.

"You're doing very well," she said honestly when their session came to an end.

He frowned at the book. "But I've got a long way to go. If you can work it into your schedule, I'd like to come on a daily basis."

It would be difficult, Meg thought. But anything to help him learn to read sooner would be worth it. He was a disruptive influence on her life and the sooner he was out of it, the better. "Daily would be fine," she agreed.

Chapter Five

Three-thirty Wednesday afternoon arrived. As the final bell of the day rang and her students fled the classroom, Meg smiled as she organized her papers and began filling her briefcase. The day had gone well. Her students had been attentive and cooperative.

Hearing the footsteps of someone entering the room, she glanced up.

"I understand that Zeke Wilson has been at your house every night since I left town," Neil said with a disapproving scowl as he approached her desk.

Meg's smile faded. "Bridge is a complicated game to learn and he has to come when he has the time," she replied levelly.

"Your home has suddenly become the focus of

every gossip in town," he continued. "And I don't like it."

Meg snapped her briefcase shut. "And I think you're exaggerating."

"Perhaps," he admitted.

Meg studied him narrowly. She'd never seen him so agitated. "Do you want to tell me what is really bothering you?" she coaxed gently.

He raked a hand through his hair. "My trip to Texas wasn't as successful as I hoped."

"You really didn't need to come back early because of me," she said feeling guilty that the gossip about Zeke had disrupted Neil's business. "I told you over the phone that Zeke has no interest in me."

"It wasn't you," he assured her. "I trust you. It's Sally. The legal matters were easy enough. I could have taken care of them from here. Sally was the reason her mother wanted me to go back to Texas with them. The girl has taken up with a most disreputable young man, by the name of Lance Verdel. Mrs. Marlow was hoping I could meet him and then talk some sense into Sally. But it was clear to me that Sally wasn't going to listen, so I ended up bringing her back here with me. Her mother and I both agreed that some distance between the two was better than doing nothing."

Meg continued to study him closely. "Didn't Sally protest?"

He shrugged a shoulder. "I told her that my mother wanted to go to New York on a shopping spree and I didn't want her going alone. I suggested to Sally that she come back with me and go with my mother, so I wouldn't have to worry about her. She's always been very fond of Mother and agreed without a fight. At least this will give Mrs. Marlow and me time to think of a new ploy to keep Sally away from that two-bit fortune hunter."

"Maybe he really cares for Sally," Meg suggested, studying Neil more closely.

Neil shook his head. "Her mother had him investigated. He woos wealthy women for their money. But usually they're older and married. It looks as if he's decided to find himself a more secure position by marrying Sally."

Meg frowned thoughtfully. "Sally has always seemed like a much too sensible girl to be taken in by a gigolo."

Neil scowled. "I always thought so, too."

"I'm sure you and your mother can talk some sense into her," Meg said encouragingly. Neil's lack of concern for her compared to his deep concern for Sally was causing a nagging suspicion to taunt Meg.

"I was hoping you might help," he coaxed. "Mother wants you to come to dinner tonight. That will give you a chance to talk with Sally...sort of woman to woman."

"I'd like that," Meg replied. She wasn't interested in having dinner with the Talmages, but she did want to watch Sally and Neil together.

Arriving home, Meg called Zeke and canceled their lesson for the evening. Then going up to her room, she dressed carefully. Neil had suggested she wear her green wool suit and she did. But as she put it on, a part of her rebelled. She did hate the way he was always telling her what to wear.

"You look like a woman with a purpose," Kate observed when Meg came downstairs to wait for Neil to arrive.

"You might say that," Meg replied.

Kate chewed nervously on her lip. "It looks to me like you figure Neil might be fixing to ask you to marry him tonight. I just hope when you become a Talmage, you won't turn into a snob like his mother."

"I promise you I won't turn into a snob like Ruth Talmage," Meg assured her.

Kate didn't look quite convinced. But she didn't say any more. Instead she rose and gave her daughter a tight hug.

"You really don't have to worry about me," Meg said as she returned her mother's hug.

Kate gave her a second hug. "Mothers are born to worry. It's in our job description."

I suppose they are, Meg thought a little while later, as she tried very hard to be fair toward Ruth Talmage.

As soon as they sat down at the dinner table, Mrs. Talmage turned her attention to Meg. "Since it is only immediate family here..." she began, then paused to glance toward Sally and smiled warmly. "We consider Sally like a daughter." The smile vanished as she again turned her attention toward Meg. "I hope you won't mind if I speak freely."

"Mother," Neil said warningly.

Ruth gave him a self-righteous glance. She was a formidable-looking woman at any time. She was always dressed in the very height of fashion. Tonight she was wearing a gown designed by a prominent Paris designer. Diamonds and pearls adorned her neck, ears and fingers. Her carefully-applied makeup hid her age well, as did her chestnut hair which—thanks to an expert hairdresser—showed no telltale signs of gray. But Ruth Talmage was even more intimidating when she felt justice was on her side, as she did at this moment. "It must be said," she insisted.

"Your mother's right," George Talmage upheld his wife's statement. He, too, seemed formidable. Tall and lean, with graying hair, he looked every bit the prosperous banker he was. "The whole family is concerned."

"What is it you want to say?" Meg questioned calmly, waiting to deny any rumors about Zeke and her and to defend her mother's right to play bridge with whomever she chose.

"You were coming along so well under my son's tutelage, my dear," Ruth continued with a sad shake of her head. "But this business with Zeke Wilson is most distressing."

The part about Neil's tutelage caused the hairs on the back of Meg's neck to bristle. But she did not let her anger show. Instead she said evenly, "I really don't understand your concern. My mother is merely teaching Zeke to play bridge."

"People will talk," Ruth replied pointedly. "If not about you and Zeke Wilson, then about your mother and Zeke Wilson."

Meg's gaze riveted on Mrs. Talmage. "What about my mother and Zeke Wilson?" she demanded.

"You have heard of this current epidemic of September-January romances or whatever people call them," Ruth replied.

"That's absurd," Meg snapped, stunned by this suggestion.

"My dear," Ruth reached over and patted Meg's hand, "we can't hide our heads in the sand. Zeke Wilson is more of the poker-playing type than the bridge-playing type. People are going to speculate."

"And I think you are overreacting, Mother," Neil interjected curtly, coming to Meg's defense.

"Neil's right," Sally spoke up. "Within the week, I suspect the gossips will have something new to interest them. Besides, we cannot allow our lives to be totally ruled by what others might think or say."

Meg saw the worried shadow pass over Neil's face and knew he was thinking about Sally's choice of companions.

"Perhaps Sally is right," George Talmage said, before his wife could launch a further protest. "And I for one do not want to destroy this delicious dinner with any further unpleasantness."

Clearly George Talmage was master of his house. Meg saw Ruth Talmage toss him a grudging glance, but she said no more about Zeke.

A tense silence began to settle over the table. Meg felt a tightening in her throat. She didn't belong here. Every fiber of her being told her so.

It was Sally who came to everyone's rescue. She began enthusiastically describing the opera she, Neil and her mother had attended in Houston.

Neil immediately joined in. Listening and watching the two of them, it occurred to Meg that they made a perfectly matched couple. They had the same social background, the same interests, even the same sense of humor.

Following the meal, Neil challenged Sally to a game of billiards. "And Meg will referee," he said. Winking mischievously at Meg, he added, "Sally tries to cheat. Someone has to be watching her every minute."

"I do not." Sally tilted her chin upward with exaggerated pride. "You're just making excuses because I win so often."

Watching the playful bantering, Meg felt like a fifth wheel.

Almost as soon as they were sequestered in the billiard room, Neil drew Meg aside. "I'm going to make an excuse and leave," he said in a whisper. "This will give you a chance to talk to Sally privately. Try to find out just how infatuated she is with this gigolo. And if you get a chance, try to talk some sense into her."

"No fair plotting with the referee," Sally protested as she began racking up the balls.

Straightening away from Meg, Neil issued an exaggerated groan. "I just remembered a phone call I've got to make," he said. "You two wait here. I won't be long."

Left alone in the room with Sally, Meg wasn't certain how to begin the probing Neil had asked her to do. But she did owe Sally a word of gratitude. "I want to thank you for coming to my aid at dinner."

"I was coming to Neil's aid," Sally replied sharply. The friendliness that had been in her voice a moment earlier was gone. Turning toward Meg, her expression was cold. "You might as well know, I've decided to fight for him."

Meg drew a deep breath. Obviously Sally had guessed that Neil had asked Meg to talk to her about Lance Verdel and she didn't like the idea. "Are you certain he's worth fighting for?" she said gently.

Sally scowled at her. "Of course Neil is worth fighting for. How can you ask such a question?"

Meg blinked in confusion. "Neil? What about the boyfriend in Houston your mother is so worried about?"

Sally scowled. "Neil told you about him?"

"He's very worried about you," Meg explained, still trying to figure out what was going on. She felt as if she had come in in the middle of a conversation.

Sally smiled triumphantly. "Good."

Meg shook her head. "I am really confused."

"It's very simple," Sally explained coolly. "I'm in love with Neil. He thinks he's in love with you. But I'm not so certain of that. He's never taken a good look at me as a woman. He still thinks of me as a little girl. And he has really enjoyed playing Henry Higgins with you."

Meg flushed. "He told you that?" she questioned sharply. She had begun to suspect this might be the case, but she didn't like the idea of the rest of the world knowing that she had allowed Neil to maneuver her toward the image he wanted to create.

Sally shrugged. "Not in so many words. But I'm not blind, and I have known Neil all my life. He likes a challenge."

"So you found a boyfriend who was totally unacceptable, so Neil would have to come to the rescue," Meg said, suddenly catching on to Sally's ploy.

"Exactly." Sally's jaw set in a hard line. "And you're not going to get him without a fight." Before Meg could respond, Sally strode out of the room.

In the next instant, Neil entered. Anger was etched into his features. "What did you say to Sally?" he demanded. "She was so upset, she wouldn't even speak to me."

"Aren't you going to ask me if she said anything to upset me?" Meg questioned levelly.

"Sally is a child and right now she's in a very fragile state," he continued agitatedly, ignoring her question. "You have probably sent her back into the arms of that gigolo."

"Sally is not a child. She is a woman and very capable of making up her own mind about what she wants to do with her life," Meg replied. The urge to get out of this house as quickly as possible overwhelmed her. "And I am getting a very bad headache. Would you please take me home?"

"I think that would be an excellent idea," he agreed, adding curtly, "before you do any more damage."

Meg refrained from making any retort. She knew now that she was dealing with a man in love. He just didn't know it. She said her goodbyes to the Talmages and Sally with polite dignity.

"I really thought you had more finesse," Neil said as he drove her home. "You'd better tell me everything you said to her so I can correct it. I just hope she doesn't take it into her mind to fly back to Houston tonight."

"I honestly didn't say anything to upset her." Meg studied the hard line of his jaw. She knew what she had to do. "You know what I think? I think you're in love with her."

Slamming on the brakes, Neil turned to stare at her. "That's preposterous!"

Having planted that seed in his mind, Meg continued, "And I resent your parents' suggestion that people might start talking about my mother and Zeke having a romantic liaison."

"They have a legitimate point," he replied coolly, releasing the brake and continuing down the street. "It doesn't look right to have Zeke Wilson hanging around your house."

"He isn't hanging around," Meg snapped.

Neil brought the car to a stop in front of Meg's home. "I never realized until now how obstinate you could be."

Meg had planned this breakup with Neil to end on a civil note, but his calling her obstinate fired her anger. She remembered Ruth Talmage's reference to "Neil's tutelage" and Sally's remark about him enjoying playing Henry Higgins and her anger grew. "And I like wearing jeans to the grocery store and the movies. I like going bowling and I hate dressing formally for dinner every evening. *And* as far as I'm concerned, whatever my mother chooses to do is just fine!"

Neil drew a terse breath. "It would seem we have quite a few irreconcilable differences."

"So it would seem," she agreed.

Neil's manner became that of a lawyer arguing a case. "Then I suppose the only reasonable thing to say is goodbye."

Meg nodded. "Goodbye," she said. Although the flash of relief she saw in Neil's eyes caused her pride to sting a bit, it was further proof that she was doing the right thing. Climbing out of the car, she walked toward the house.

She heard Neil driving off as she opened the front door. Glancing over her shoulder, she saw Lucile Tate's curtains swing quickly closed. By mid-morning everyone in town would know she and Neil had fought.

"You're home early," Kate said, coming out of the den to greet her daughter.

"I broke up with Neil," Meg replied simply. She expected to feel a certain amount of depression. After all, she had wanted a home and children of her own. Instead she felt only relief.

"Good." Kate nodded her head. "Never did like the way he was trying to change you to suit his family." She suddenly smiled brightly. "Jane's nephew is coming for a visit."

Meg frowned. "The one who used to catch beetles and put them down my shirt when we were kids?"

"That's the one," Kate confirmed. "He became an entomologist and works for the Department of Agriculture. He's got a real good job *and* he isn't married."

"I'm not surprised," Meg muttered, recalling the gleeful laughter her screams and squirming used to elicit from the boy.

"I'm sure he's grown into a very nice young man," Kate insisted. "I'll invite him over for dinner one night."

Meg knew the look on her mother's face. It would do no good to ask her to refrain from matchmaking.

"Maybe he's changed," she mused philosophically, as she climbed into bed a little while later.

Slowly a single tear trickled down her cheek. She didn't regret breaking up with Neil. It had been the right thing to do. But she did want a family of her own.

Chapter Six

"Heard you and Neil broke up," Zeke said as he followed Meg into the living room the next evening to begin his lesson.

That morning when Meg pulled out of the driveway and started down the street on her way to school, she had seen Lucile Tate hurrying across the road. She knew Lucile was going to quiz Kate about what had happened between Meg and Neil. She also knew that as soon as Lucile found out about the breakup, the news would spread quickly. But Meg didn't care. She felt as if a two-ton weight had been lifted off her shoulders.

"True," she replied.

"I thought I might have been the cause of your misunderstanding, so I went to see him today. Planned to tell him the real reason I was spending so much time over here," Zeke continued. "But he wasn't interested in talking to me. He said I didn't have anything to do with the breakup. I also got the impression it was permanent."

Meg looked at him in surprise. She hadn't expected Zeke Wilson to try to come to her rescue. "You didn't have anything to do with it," she assured him, adding with finality, "and it is permanent."

Zeke had remained standing. Hooking his thumbs through the belt loops on his jeans, he studied her intently. "You don't seem too upset, or are you just real good at hiding your feelings?"

"It's for the best," she replied. Having no intention of discussing her love life or lack of it with Zeke Wilson, she added in her best teacher's voice, "Now shall we get on with your lesson?"

But Zeke didn't move. "No matter what you and Neil say, people are going to blame me for your split. I figure I deserve to know what broke up the two of you."

She faced him coldly. "You don't deserve to know anything. This doesn't involve you, at all."

A cynical smile tilted one corner of his mouth. "What happened? You decide having his money wasn't worth sharing his bed?"

Meg's cheeks flamed in anger. "I told you I wasn't interested in his money."

He continued to regard her cynically. "But you were considering marrying him. If you didn't love him— and, in view of your less-than-brokenhearted attitude, it's my guess that you didn't—and if you weren't interested in his money, why would you want to marry him?''

His sarcastic manner made it clear he didn't believe her disclaimer about not being interested in Neil's money. Pride demanded that she defend herself. ''I liked him and I thought he would be a good husband and father,'' she replied with cool dignity. ''I want to have children before it's too late, and I'm old-fashioned enough to feel the need to have a husband to go with them.''

''I would have thought Talmage would fit those requirements nicely,'' Zeke persisted, his voice implying he still didn't believe her.

Meg faced him defiantly. ''He kept trying to change me to suit his taste, and I like me the way I am. Also I'm fairly certain he's in love with Sally Marlow. He just doesn't know it yet. And I know she's in love with him.''

Zeke continued to study her skeptically. ''And so you simply bowed out of the picture to let true love run its course?''

''Yes,'' she snapped. ''And I'm finished discussing my private life with you. It's none of your business, anyway.'' She couldn't believe she had been so open with him. Furious with herself, she added pointedly, ''And I don't expect you to repeat anything I've told you.''

He scowled. ''I'm not a gossip.''

''You could have fooled me,'' she returned snidely. ''You're better at cross-examining a person than Lucile Tate, and she's an expert. Now if you want to have a lesson, let's get on with it, or you can leave."

Giving a nonchalant shrug, as if he suddenly found discussing her private life boring, Zeke sat down at the table and opened the text they were using.

Seating herself, Meg couldn't believe she had let him goad her into making so many personal confessions. Well, he was good practice for what was to come over the next few days, she reasoned philosophically. Next time she'd be a great deal more discreet.

The lesson finally ended and she breathed a sigh of relief as Zeke rose to leave. But at the door he paused and turned back to face her. "What are your plans, now that Neil is out of the picture?"

She glared at his impudence. "That is really none of your business."

He regarded her with narrowed eyes. "I just wondered if you were going to be leaving town in search of greener fields for husband-hunting. If you are I'll have to find a new teacher."

"I'll let you know," she replied dryly.

He nodded, turned and left.

The moment he was gone, Kate came in. "I was wondering the same thing myself," she said.

"Same 'what' thing?" Meg asked, picking up the texts and stacking them carefully in the bookcase.

"What are you going to do now that Neil is out of the picture?" Kate elaborated.

"I don't know," Meg answered honestly. "Maybe Jane's nephew will turn out to be Mr. Right, or maybe I'll look for a job in Kansas City. Or take a cruise. I'd like to think there is someone out there for me somewhere." She shrugged and smiled crookedly. "Or maybe I'll just stay here and drift quietly into spinsterhood. I have a career I enjoy. You and I get along well, and I like living here in Vincent's Gap."

Kate shook her head. "Spinsterhood is out. I want some grandchildren. I'll find you a husband, if it's the last thing I do."

Meg groaned. "I'd rather do it myself."

Kate ignored her daughter's plea. "I'm going to make a list right now. There's Clare's grandson. I'm sure she won't mind inviting him for a weekend so the two of you can meet."

Meg watched her mother leave the room.

Sinking into the couch she stared at the line of family pictures on the mantel. "Why me?" she demanded. "Why did I have to inherit this strong nesting instinct? Some women lead wonderful, fulfilling lives without ever feeling any need for a cozy little home and children. I have a good career, and I'm not interested in a man to take care of me. I can take very good care of myself." A hopeful look came to her face. "Maybe I should get a dog or a cat."

Kate came back into the room with a pad of paper and a pencil. "I've already thought of four possibilities," she announced cheerfully.

"And I've got papers to grade," Meg said, rising and moving toward the door before her mother could begin to give details. On the way up the stairs, she promised herself she would look into getting a pet.

* * *

The next morning, as she sat at the breakfast table listening to her mother list the names of available males, Meg found herself seriously trying to decide between a dog and a cat.

A knock on the back door interrupted Kate's dissertation. Relieved to have a reprieve, Meg answered it to find Lucile Tate on the other side.

Entering, the woman took Meg's hand and gave it a motherly squeeze. "I just couldn't let you start your day without warning you," she said.

"Would you like a cup of coffee, Lucile?" Kate offered, already pouring a cup.

Looking around Meg, Lucile smiled. "That would be nice." Then returning her attention to Meg, her expression became that of a person bearing news of doom. "Maggie Banck called me last night. I'm sure you've seen her up at the Talmage house. She works as a day maid. Anyway, she called me last night. Seems that Neil went to New York with his mother and that Sally Marlow woman." Sympathy entered Lucile's voice. "Maggie said he went along to buy an engagement ring for Miss Marlow."

"He's getting engaged so quickly?" Kate questioned sharply, glancing protectively toward Meg. "Why, that cad! He must have been seeing that Marlow woman behind Meg's back."

"Neil did nothing wrong and I wish them the best," Meg interrupted before her mother could say more.

Lucile frowned with disbelief. "You really shouldn't have let him get away so easily," she admonished. "At your age, you're not going to get too many choices."

Meg knew the woman was only saying what the rest of the town would be thinking. Beneath her calm exterior, she cringed. This was not going to be a good day. She didn't mind the gossip behind her back, but she hated the sympathetic glances that would be cast in her direction.

Kate dumped the cup of coffee she had just poured into the sink. "I think it would be best if you went home," she said, her expression warning Lucile that this was an order, not a request.

"I'm just concerned about Meg's future," Lucile replied with self-righteous indignation. She did move toward the door, but when she was half in and half out the doorway, she paused. Looking back at Kate, she added sternly, "You should be concerned, too. At this rate Meg's going to end up a spinster."

Kate's face flushed scarlet with anger, but before she could offer a response Lucile had completed her exit and was scurrying down the drive. Drawing a deep, calming breath, Kate turned to her daughter. "I'm sorry about that. Lucile never knows when to stop." Anger again flashed in her eyes. "To be perfectly honest, I never did like Neil. But I never thought he would do a thing like this to you."

While it was going to make her look like a naive fool, in all fairness Meg couldn't blame Neil. "He didn't know how he felt about Sally until I told him,'' she said in his defense.

Kate frowned in confusion. "You told him?"

"I know it's going to be a bit embarrassing for the next couple of days, but it's for the best," Meg assured her mother.

"I suppose." Kate's expression brightened. "At least I don't have to worry about you becoming a snob." A gleam entered her eyes. "And I'm having coffee this morning with Jane. I want to make some discreet inquiries about her nephew."

Meg groaned aloud, but Kate ignored it.

Driving to work, Meg hoped the news of Neil's departure for New York had not spread too swiftly. Her prayers weren't answered. Gail Gytha, the principal's secretary, greeted her with the sympathetic smile she usually reserved for teachers being called in for a reprimand or someone who had learned he had a terminal illness.

In the teacher's lounge, Meg was met by encouraging smiles from her co-workers. "Well, at least you won't have to worry about having Ruth Talmage as a mother-in-law," Barbara Bradley, the home-economics teacher said, trying to lighten the tension that had suddenly filled the room when Meg entered.

Meg agreed with a cheerful smile, but the looks on the faces of those present told her that they didn't believe her. They simply thought she was putting up a good front. Wishing she had settled for a dog or cat weeks earlier, she escaped to her classroom.

Chapter Seven

"At least my students were in a learning mood today," she said with a sigh as she drove home that afternoon. "And it's Friday!" By Monday, she knew, people would once again be concerned with their own problems and her impending spinsterhood would have faded from their minds.

Nearing her home, she saw Zeke Wilson's pickup parked in front. *He probably has a date and wants to get his lesson over with early,* she decided, gathering up her books and papers. The thought produced a tiny twinge in her abdomen and she scowled at herself. She and Zeke Wilson mixed like oil and water. *And he'd better not ask any more personal questions!* she thought as she walked toward the house.

Zeke and her mother were sitting at the kitchen table when Meg entered. "I'm teaching Zeke the finer points of bidding," Kate said, glancing up and smiling a welcome. "He's doing so well, I'm seriously considering signing us up for the next tournament."

Meg forced a tired smile. Then turning her attention to Zeke she said, "Can I assume you're here because you want to get our session over with for today?"

"Yes," he replied. Thanking Kate for the bridge lesson he headed toward the living room.

But when Meg joined him a few minutes later, he wasn't sitting at the card table going over the text. Instead he was standing staring out the front window.

As she closed the door he turned to face her. "I didn't come here for a lesson," he said stiffly. "I've been thinking about what you said last night."

"Stop right there," she warned. "You're my student and I'm your teacher. My personal life is my business, not yours. I thought we settled that last night."

His jaw hardened in a determined line. "I've come here to ask you to marry me."

"You what?" she demanded, adding in shocked disbelief, "You don't even like me."

Surprise registered on his face. "I like you just fine."

The disbelief remained on her face. "Well you sure haven't acted that way."

"I admit you make me uneasy," he admitted self-consciously. "You're an educated woman and I'm an uneducated man. I suppose that intimidated me a little, and I don't like feeling intimidated."

"You were intimidated by me?" she questioned incredulously.

"Still am a little," he replied. "I'm used to women who react to life on a more emotional level." His face took on a coolly businesslike expression as he continued, "But the more I thought about it, the more I liked your practical approach to marriage. I'm not a big believer in falling in love. Seems to me that love just causes a lot of trouble for the man and woman involved. My dad loved my mom. After she died, he was never happy. He grieved for her the rest of his life. Through the years I've watched my friends falling in and out of love . . . getting married, getting divorced. They spend more time miserable than happy. I decided a long time ago that none of that was for me."

"In other words, you don't believe in letting anyone get too close. That way you can't get hurt," Meg mused.

"I just don't believe in looking for misery," he replied dryly. "Anyway, as I was saying, I've worked hard all my life and don't have any close family to leave what I've built to. I'd like to have an heir or two. The way I see it, we could have a mutually beneficial marriage. You could have the children you want. I would have heirs. You could continue to teach me to read, and if Joan wants to retire earlier than she planned, she can teach you how to keep the books and you can teach me. I can't provide you with all the luxuries Talmage could have provided you with, but I can support you in a reasonably comfortable style. It's a practical arrangement that would solve all of our problems.''

''That is probably the most cynical proposal a woman has ever had,'' Meg muttered, still having trouble believing this was really happening.

He regarded her calmly. ''You were going to marry Talmage and you didn't love him. Or were you lying when you said you weren't interested in the luxuries a man could offer you?''

She glared at him in indignation. ''I wasn't lying about that.''

''But you're not interested in hooking up with an uneducated farmer, either. Sorry I wasted your time.'' He started toward the door, but Meg blocked his exit.

''You have the most infuriating habit of asking a person something and then making his decision for him,'' she said angrily. ''You come in here and out of the clear blue sky you ask me to marry you. Don't you think it would be reasonable to assume I'd need some time to adjust to the idea? Don't you think the polite thing for you to do would be to offer me time to think about it? Or did you suddenly change your mind and decide it was a bad idea, after all?''

''I didn't decide it was a bad idea,'' he replied stiffly. Continuing to regard her grimly, he asked, ''Are you interested in considering it?''

She was prepared to say no. She was prepared to tell him that she had stopped him because she was tired of the way he walked out on her without letting her explain her reasons. But instead she heard herself saying, "Maybe." *You're crazy!* her inner voice screamed. *But it would be a practical solution,* she found herself countering.

"Then you think about it and let me know when you've made a decision," he said gruffly. Placing his hands on her upper arms, he gently but firmly moved her out of his way and left the room.

Going over to the window, Meg watched him walking to his truck. She could still feel a lingering warmth on her arms where he had touched her. Remembering the sensations she'd experienced in his embrace when he guided her around the dance floor, a rush of excitement swept through her. At least the physical attraction would be there.

"That was a fast lesson," Kate said, entering the room. "You and Zeke didn't have a quarrel, did you? He seemed a little uneasy today and you've been on edge lately. I'd hate to have anything happen between the two of you that would stop him from coming to learn to read."

"We didn't quarrel," Meg answered, watching the blue pickup drive away.

"I'm glad to hear that," Kate rattled on. "I admire him for trying to better himself."

"I do, too," Meg admitted.

"It's a shame he's such a confirmed bachelor," Kate continued thoughtfully. "Of course the two of you seem to mix like oil and water."

See, even your mother realizes that a marriage between you and Zeke would be ridiculous, Meg's inner voice pointed out.

She could be wrong, she argued back.

But was it worth taking the chance?

"Jane's nephew is definitely out of the question," Kate announced with a snort. "When I went over there today, she showed me a paperweight he sent her for Christmas. I've never seen anything so awful. It was a huge beetle. Ugly-looking thing. Never knew they grew so large. It could have carried away this entire house. Anyway it was encased in plastic. He'd sent along a note telling her that he'd caught it just for her. *And* she told me that he has glass cases of bugs all over his apartment. She says it gives her the creeps to go visit him. Besides, I don't want a son-in-law who will send me bugs for presents."

"I agree," Meg replied, continuing to stare out the window. The truth was that, in spite of her reservations, the temptation to accept Zeke's proposal was growing strong with each passing moment. It was a practical solution to her dilemma. *A dog or a cat would be more practical,* her inner voice argued.

But not as fulfilling, she argued back.

"You don't even know what you agreed to," Kate scolded. "You haven't been paying the least bit of attention to me."

Meg turned toward her mother. "You said that Jane's nephew has an apartment full of bugs and gets them encased in paperweights to give away as Christmas gifts." Turning back to stare out the window, her mouth formed a thoughtful pout. She and Zeke would have as good a chance as any couple to make their marriage work. Maybe better. They wouldn't be going into it dewy-eyed. They both knew openly and up front what each wanted from the union.

"But I'm not giving up," Kate continued. "I'm going over to Nan's tomorrow. Her grandson just graduated from medical school. He was living with a girl, but they broke up."

"Don't bother." Turning back toward her mother, Meg said levelly, "Zeke asked me to marry him."

Kate stared at her daughter in surprise. "He what?"

"He asked me to marry him," Meg repeated, already moving toward the door.

"Wait," Kate followed her daughter down the hall and through the kitchen. "Where are you going?"

"To accept," Meg replied, grabbing her coat, purse and keys without breaking stride. Pausing with her hand on the door, she turned back toward her mother and added, "I think." Then she left.

Three times on the way out to Zeke's farm, she almost turned around and went home. Guiding her car up his long driveway, she told herself this was crazy. But when she thought about sharing his bed, a nervous excitement stirred within her. All her life she'd been practical and levelheaded. Maybe it was time to take a chance.

Zeke opened the door at the same moment she raised her hand to knock. "I saw you coming up the drive," he said in response to her startled reaction. "Come in."

He stepped aside and she entered. The house had a decidedly masculine feel to it. He motioned her toward the living room. The furniture was Early American in style. It looked used but not tattered.

Too nervous to sit, she stood in front of the fireplace. On the mantel was a picture of a young boy being held on his mother's lap. The child was smiling with abandon. Meg looked back at the man that boy had become and wondered if he ever smiled like that now.

"Do you have an answer for me already?" he asked when she didn't speak.

"I have a few questions first," she replied.

"What do you want to know?" he asked, his manner strictly businesslike.

"I guess they aren't really questions," she said, trying to sound as composed as he did. "They are sort of conditions."

He continued to regard her stoically. "What conditions, then?"

"I intend to keep my job until the first child is born," she replied.

"If that is what you want, it's fine with me," he agreed, then added, "I hire Ida Crammer to come in and clean once a week. I'll continue to retain her services. You would be coming here as my wife, not my maid."

"I appreciate that," she said. Her shoulders straightened with pride as she prepared to make her final demand. "Also, I will not be made to look like a fool. You will be faithful to me for as long as we are married."

"I will abide by the marriage vows in every way," he assured her.

She held out her hand toward him in the manner of one shaking on a deal that has been set. "Then you have yourself a wife," she replied. "A fiancée," she corrected quickly.

"Fine," he replied, accepting the handshake.

The warmth of his touch traveled up her arm. Slipping her hand out of his, she said, "Mom and I will be eating dinner around seven. You're invited."

His expression was shuttered as he continued to watch her. "I'll be there."

"I'll see you at a little before seven, then." Nervously she walked toward the door. She wished he would make a move to kiss her. It seemed like the proper thing to do at a moment like this. But he didn't. *You and Zeke have an agreement, not a love match,* she reminded herself tersely.

As she drove away from the house, she glanced in the rearview mirror. He was still standing in the doorway, his expression grim. *It just doesn't feel right that a proposal and the acceptance of that proposal should be handled in so cold a manner,* she thought. Of course she had to admit that she was half to blame. Suddenly slamming on the brakes, she threw the car into reverse and backed up the drive.

Zeke came down from the porch as she came to a halt.

Climbing out of the car, she stood in front of him, her hands on her hips. "I believe you were supposed to kiss me. You proposed . . . maybe it wasn't a conventional proposal. I accepted...maybe it wasn't a conventional acceptance. But you did and I did, and we're going to get married, and you should have kissed me.''

A flicker of amusement shown in the dark depths of his eyes. ''You were the one who wanted to shake hands. I was merely following your lead.''

She frowned self-consciously. ''I was nervous. I knew we should do something, I just wasn't certain...'' The sentence died as he cupped her face in her hands.

''You're right,'' he said gruffly. ''I should have kissed you.''

Very softly he kissed one corner of her mouth. ''Thank you,'' he said. He kissed the other corner of her mouth. ''For accepting my proposal.''

Meg's blood raced through her veins. ''You're welcome,'' she replied shakily.

He smiled and claimed her mouth fully. It was a gentle contact at first, but Meg's lips felt as if they were being touched by smoldering fire. Her hands moved upward over his chest. The feel of the hard musculature of his body beneath her palms awakened sensations deep within her she had never before experienced. They were both frightening and exciting at the same time.

Releasing her face, he drew her into his embrace and as her arms circled his neck, he deepened the kiss.

Meg found herself wishing she wasn't wearing a coat, wishing she could feel the length of his body without the cloth barrier between them. Shocked by the wantonness of her thoughts, she loosened her hold.

Dropping light kisses on her lips, he released her slowly.

Her hands trailed over his shoulders and down his chest as he stepped back from her. Chewing on the inside of her bottom lip, she met his dark gaze.

"Did I do it right this time, teacher?" he asked, huskily.

"You did very nicely," she managed to reply. Shaken by how strong her physical attraction for him was, she stepped back toward her car. "See you at seven," she said, and with a calm she didn't feel, she climbed in behind the wheel and drove away.

At least we shouldn't have any trouble in the bedroom, she thought, her blood still racing.

Kate was waiting for her when Meg returned home. "Well?" she demanded as Meg entered the kitchen.

"I accepted," Meg replied.

Kate shook her head. "I don't understand any of this."

Meg considered lying to her mother, telling her that she and Zeke were in love. But she'd never been good at fabrication, and she'd never been able to lie successfully to Kate. Looking at her mother pleadingly, she said, "All you need to understand is that I want this marriage to take place and I want your blessing."

Kate studied her daughter with a worried frown. "You've concocted some sort of deal with him about him fathering your children in exchange for you teaching him to read, haven't you?"

"No," Meg replied firmly. "We simply discovered that we both have a great many of the same goals and we feel we can have a good marriage."

Kate's frown deepened. "That sounds a little too modern for my taste."

"Actually it's very old-fashioned," Meg rebutted. "In the past, the majority of marriages were arranged. We merely arranged this one ourselves without the help of a matchmaker."

"But how do you feel about him as a man?" Kate's cheeks flushed slightly. "You are going to be sharing his bed."

Again an excitement stirred within Meg. "I find him physically appealing," she admitted levelly.

"And you're determined to go through with this?" Kate questioned.

Meg's shoulders straightened with determination. "Yes."

"You could do worse," Kate admitted, still looking worried. She gave her daughter a tight hug. "If it's what you want, you have my blessing. I just hope it works out the way you want it to."

I hope so, too, Meg prayed silently as she returned her mother's hug. Straightening away from Kate, she said, "I invited him for dinner. He should be arriving a little before seven."

Kate's jaw tensed. "Good."

Meg knew that look meant trouble. "Mom, please," she begged. "Just give him your blessing."

"Even if you told me you were madly in love with the man, there'd be a few questions I'd feel I had to ask," Kate replied.

From the set of her mother's jaw, Meg knew that no pleading would change Kate's mind. *If Zeke decides to call the whole thing off because of my mother's cross-examination, then we would never have made it through the first month of the marriage anyway,* she told herself philosophically. But that didn't keep her nerves from tensing painfully. They were as tight as violin strings by the time the clock read 6:45.

As the minutes ticked slowly by and Zeke did not arrive, Meg's stomach began to knot. The thought that he had changed his mind about wanting to marry her began to taunt her.

The look on Kate's face as the grandfather clock in the hallway began to chime seven told Meg that her mother had the same thought.

The knot in Meg's stomach grew tighter. Obviously when he'd kissed her he hadn't had the reaction she'd had. The kiss had left him cold and he'd decided he didn't want her in his bed. It's probably for the best, she told herself, trying to ignore the feelings of embarrassment and humiliation that threatened to overwhelm her. The marriage probably wouldn't have worked, anyway. Hadn't she told herself it was a crazy idea from the start?

But as the echo of the seventh chime faded, she heard the sound of Zeke's truck.

Parking in front, he strode quickly toward the house.

Watching him from the window, Meg couldn't help worrying that his tardiness was due to second thoughts he was suddenly having about the marriage. She promised herself she would give him the opportunity to back out of it before he faced her mother. Forcing herself to wait until he knocked, she walked out into the hall and answered the door.

"Sorry I'm late," he apologized as she took his coat and hung it in the closet.

Turning to face him, she asked with calm dignity, "Are you certain you want to go through with this marriage?"

His expression became grim. "Is that a polite way of telling me that you have changed your mind?"

For a moment, she was tempted to say yes. She couldn't stop thinking that she was asking for trouble if she continued with this arrangement. But she didn't. She wanted to marry him. "I was merely giving you one last opportunity to back out. I thought you might be late because you were having doubts."

He traced the line of her jaw with the tip of his finger. "I'm not interested in backing out."

Meg saw the flicker of desire in his eyes and felt a responding fire begin to burn within her.

"Now that you two have that settled, I'd like to ask Zeke a few questions," Kate said, coming out into the hall.

Meg flushed as she realized her mother had been listening in from the dining room. Well, she'd told Kate that this wasn't a marriage based on love. "Won't dinner get cold?" she asked pointedly, making an attempt to delay her mother's cross-examination for a while.

"I made a pot roast. It can sit for another half an hour without any problem," Kate replied.

"I'm sorry I'm late," Zeke apologized to Kate as she came to a halt in front of him.

Kate ignored his apology. "I don't know what this is all about," she said, studying him with a narrowed gaze. "But Meg tells me that she wants to marry you, and she's old enough to make her own decisions. However, I knew your dad was a man of his word and folks say you are, too, so I want your word that you'll treat her well."

Meg flushed with embarrassment. "Mother!"

"It's a fair request," Zeke replied, showing no offense. Holding out his hand toward Kate, he said, "You have my word."

Kate accepted the handshake as a sign of his bond. "Then you have my blessing."

As Meg drew a relieved sigh, Zeke opened the closet and reached into the pocket of his coat. "This was why I was late," he said, handing a jeweler's ring box to Meg. "It took me a while to find it and then I wanted to take it by the jeweler's and have it cleaned."

Opening the box, Meg gasped. The ring inside was obviously old. A medium-sized diamond was set in an ornate spun-gold mounting with two smaller diamonds encased on either side. "It's beautiful."

"It was my grandmother's," Zeke explained.

"It is gorgeous," Kate confirmed, as Meg held the box so her mother could see the ring better.

"I can have the diamonds put in a more modern setting if you want," Zeke offered.

"No." Meg shook her head. "It's lovely just the way it is."

"Maybe we should see if it fits," he suggested, when she continued to hold the box without touching the ring. Taking it out of its velvet entrapment, he slipped it on her finger. It fit perfectly.

"It's so beautiful," Meg repeated, unable to think of anything else to say. She hadn't expected him to give her a family heirloom. She'd expected something more impersonal. But then, today had been a day of surprises.

Zeke smiled crookedly. "I believe you're supposed to kiss me for it."

"I'll just go set dinner on the table," Kate said, slipping quickly out of the hall.

Meg barely noticed her mother's exit. Rising up on tiptoes, she gently cupped Zeke's face in her hands. "Thank you," she said softly, as her lips found his.

She'd meant it to be a light kiss, but the feel of his mouth on hers was too inviting to resist. Her hands moved to the back of his neck, her fingers entwining in his thick, dark hair, as she drew his head closer to hers for a firmer contact.

Zeke's arms circled her and she let her body mold softly against his. As if there was no barrier of clothing between them, she felt his strength, his warmth. Her blood raced hot through her veins.

Suddenly embarrassed by the wantonness of her body's reaction to him, she forced herself to slowly release him and back out of his arms. "I'd better go help my mother put dinner on the table," she said a little shakily.

Before she could turn away, he caught her chin with the tips of his fingers and placed a light kiss on the tip of her nose. "You do know how to thank a man," he said gruffly. "This marriage is going to work out just fine."

Silently Meg hoped he was right.

"Have you talked about a date for the wedding?" Kate asked when they were all seated at the table. "Spring weddings are nice."

"I was sort of thinking of a fall wedding. Say in about two weeks," Zeke replied.

Meg, who was serving herself some peas, paused in mid-motion and stared at him in surprise. "Two weeks?"

"Don't see any reason for a long engagement," he replied. "But if that's what you want, it's fine with me."

Forcing her arm to move, she finished putting the peas on her plate. There really wasn't any reason for a long engagement. Setting the bowl of peas down, she met his gaze levelly. "Two weeks is fine with me."

"That's going to be a little rushed for making the arrangements," Kate interjected, looking disturbed by the swiftness with which they intended to proceed.

"I always planned to wear your wedding gown," Meg pointed out. "It shouldn't need too many alterations. I thought I'd ask you to be my attendant and you can wear something you already own if you want to. Or we can go into Kansas City for a day and you can find something new. The men in the wedding can wear suits. We'll keep the guest list small, just family and close friends." Suddenly realizing that she'd taken it upon herself to outline the plans for their wedding without consulting Zeke, she turned to him and said with a touch of embarrassment, "If that's all right with you."

"Sounds fine to me," he agreed.

Kate looked dubiously from one to the other. "If you're sure that's what you want."

Zeke nodded his consent.

"It's what we want," Meg confirmed.

Kate continued to study them for a moment longer, then began serving herself. "Maybe it's just as well," she said as she passed the plate of meat. "This marriage is bound to cause a lot of gossip. The sooner it's accomplished, the sooner everyone can move on to minding someone else's business." Pausing as she dished herself some potatoes, her gaze traveled pointedly from Meg to Zeke. "And you might as well know, I plan to tell everyone that the two of you are in love . . . that you're absolutely crazy about one another. *And* I don't expect either of you to contradict me."

"I wouldn't consider crossing you," Zeke assured her with a hint of amusement in his eyes.

It occurred to Meg that *crazy* was an excellent word to describe this situation, but she kept that thought to herself.

Chapter Eight

Saturday dawned crisp and bright. As soon as Meg and Kate finished breakfast, they started working on plans for the wedding. Meg tried on her mother's dress and called Gail James to come over and do alterations on it.

Zeke came by after Gail left and he and Meg went to see the minister to set up an actual date for the wedding. Rev. Howard's usual unrufflable demeanor slipped when they explained the purpose of their visit.

"You two want to get married to one another?" he questioned in disbelief.

"Yes," Zeke answered firmly.

"I think we should talk," the reverend said, motioning them into the two chairs that faced his desk. Seating himself, he studied them more calmly. "I've known the both of you for nearly fifteen years. In all that time, I feel safe in saying that neither of you has ever acted irrationally nor made any important decision on a whim.''

"And we haven't this time," Zeke assured him.

"I really must point out that the two of you were dating other people up to a week ago," the minister persisted. "Now you tell me you want to be married in two weeks. I don't want to talk you out of getting married, but I do think it would be prudent to give yourselves a little more time. It has been my experience that love is an emotion that needs time to grow." Clearing his throat nervously, his gaze traveled from Zeke to Meg. "There is no delicate way to put this. Sometimes couples mistake lust for love. When the passion dies, and it will without the foundation of love, the marriage falls apart.''

Meg shifted nervously in her chair. What if he asked her directly if she was in love with Zeke? She couldn't lie to her minister.

Reaching across the small space between them, Zeke took her hand in his. "Meg and I know what our feelings are." The "Don't Tread on Me" look Meg remembered from fifth grade came over his face. "Will you marry us or do we have to go to a justice of the peace?''

Rev. Howard studied Meg narrowly. "Are you as certain about this as Zeke is?" he questioned.

She felt the warmth of Zeke's hand traveling up her arm. "Yes," she replied.

Rev. Howard continued to look dubious, but he set the date.

Leaving the church, they made a trip to the florist.

"If I see one more shocked stare, I'll scream," Meg told her mother as the three of them sat making out a guest list later that evening.

"Well, you have to expect people to be a bit surprised. A week ago you were at a dance with Neil," Kate pointed out in a reasoning voice.

"Rev. Howard mentioned the same thing," Meg admitted. Glancing over at Zeke, it was hard to believe that it was barely a week since he'd come uninvited into her life. Now he was going to become a permanent part of it. *Unless he gets bored with the arrangement and wants out,* her little voice interjected. After all, he didn't love her. *No two people can go into marriage one-hundred-percent certain it will work out the way they expect,* she argued back. For the umpteenth time she told herself that they had as good a chance as any.

The next morning she got her mother up a little earlier than usual. "I have to watch over the nursery again today," she explained when Kate protested.

"You want to get to church and hide yourself down there before the crowds begin to arrive," Kate corrected, reading her daughter like a book.

"You're right," Meg confessed. "Now get up."

She had dressed and was in the kitchen pouring herself a cup of coffee when a knock sounded on the back door. It was Lucile Tate.

"I had to come over and offer my congratulations," Lucile gushed as she entered the kitchen. "I just knew Zeke Wilson wasn't spending all his time over here to learn bridge from Kate. I told everyone it just didn't make any sense for a man like him to suddenly want to join our stodgy little group. Tell me, was he the reason you and Neil broke up?"

"Neil and I were never that serious about one another," Meg replied. "We were just friends."

"It was kismet when she and Zeke were suddenly brought together," Kate interjected, entering the kitchen at that point. "I asked her to help me teach him to play bridge. Almost as soon as they sat down together, I could see the attraction was there."

"He is quite a hunk," Lucile admitted. "But I have to confess, I never thought he was the marrying kind and I would never have matched him with Meg."

"Well, you know what they say about opposites attracting," Meg hedged. "Now I really have to be getting to the church." Taking Lucile by the arm, Meg nearly shoved her out the back door. She knew that what the woman was saying was what most people in town were thinking, and she didn't want to participate in the same conversation two or three dozen times. She wanted to get to church and hide herself in the nursery.

But her plan didn't work. Lucile's visit had slowed them down and Kate had trouble getting her hair to look right. By the time they arrived at church, half the congregation was already there. Zeke was there, too. Janet Vees and Emily Crebs were with him. Meg's stomach threatened to knot. She knew both women had been after Zeke for years and he'd dated each of them a couple of times. Taking a deep breath, she told herself that she was not jealous.

Seeing her, Zeke waved and started across the lawn in her direction. Behind him, Meg saw the pouts on Emily and Janet's face. If Zeke wanted to stray, he wouldn't have far to look for companionship. Again her stomach threatened to knot.

"It's about time you two showed up," he growled in low tones for their ears only as he reached them. "Never knew my getting married could be of so much interest to other people."

Meg was tempted to say that it looked to her as if he hadn't minded the company he'd been keeping. But she held her tongue.

"Meg, dear," a woman's honeyed tones sounded from behind her.

Recognizing the voice, Meg paled slightly. Schooling her face into a polite smile, she turned. "Good morning, Mrs. Talmage."

Ruth Talmage's normal regal bearing was even more pronounced today. Like a queen speaking to a lowly subject, she said with patronizing benevolence, "I understand congratulations are in order."

"Thank you," Meg replied, her guard in place. Ruth Talmage was a woman who liked having the last word. Meg had hoped not to have to face her for a few more days. Unable to totally hide her surprise at finding Mrs. Talmage back in Vincent's Gap so quickly, she couldn't keep herself from saying, "I thought you would still be in New York."

"Oh, no, dear." Ruth's smile brightened. "As soon as the ring was picked out, Neil and Sally flew to Houston so that he could speak to her father and make their engagement official." Ruth Talmage's voice normally carried well. But today she raised it even further so that several of the surrounding groups could distinctly hear what she had to say. "I'm so glad you and Neil were both able to find partners who are much more well-suited to your stations in life."

Meg had endured Ruth Talmage's barbs for months. Facing the woman with dignity, she said with honest relief, "So am I. Please give Neil and Sally my very best wishes."

Kate smiled smugly as Ruth snorted indignantly and walked away.

"I really have to be getting to the nursery," Meg insisted, wanting to get away before anyone else could approach.

Zeke offered her his arm. "I'll walk you there."

Meg glanced questioningly toward her mother.

"You two run along," Kate said in answer to her daughter's glance. "I want to check with Claire about baking your wedding cake. She makes the best ones in these parts." And with a quick wave, she headed toward a group gathered near the entrance to the sanctuary.

Skirting the main entrance, Meg headed toward a side door that led to the rooms in the basement. Zeke accompanied her in stoic silence, and she again found herself wondering if he was considering changing his mind about the marriage.

As Meg entered the nursery, Susan Howard, the minister's wife, breathed a sigh of relief. "I'm so glad you're here." Then seeing Zeke enter, she smiled brightly. "Congratulations, you two." The smile vanished and her expression became apologetic as she quickly shifted her attention back to Meg. "I hate to do this to you, Meg," she said in hurried tones. "But Ellen called this morning. She has the flu. You'll have to do the nursery alone. I'd stay and help, but I've got a solo this morning and I should be in the choir room practicing now." Handing Meg the baby she'd been rocking, Susan practically raced through the door.

"I'll stay and help," Zeke said, closing the door so that the two little ones crawling on the floor couldn't make an escape.

"There isn't any need," Meg assured him, shifting the baby into a more comfortable position. "I can handle this on my own."

He regarded her grimly. "I might as well get a little practice."

She saw the anger that flashed in his eyes and was certain he was suddenly feeling trapped. Pride caused her shoulders to stiffen. If he wanted out of the marriage, then she would let him out.

Two more couples brought their babies in, and as each one congratulated them Meg watched Zeke closely. He smiled each time, but the smile never reached his eyes.

She waited until the faint tones of the first hymn being sung in the service reached them. She didn't want anyone walking in and hearing what she had to say. The baby she was holding had fallen asleep and, lying it down, she covered it with a light blanket, then turned to face Zeke.

He was watching the two younger babies who were still in the crawling stage chasing after the one toddler in the room. The gentleness in his eyes contrasted sharply with the hard set of his jaw. *They're fun to watch but he doesn't really want any of his own,* she thought tersely.

"You've been acting like a man who feels trapped. If you want out of the marriage all you have to do is say so," she said stiffly.

The gentleness left his eyes as his gaze swung toward her. "I don't want out," he assured her. "But there is one thing we need to get straight. It has occurred to me over the past couple of days I might have given you the wrong impression about any children we might have. I don't intend to simply sire them and then turn them over to you. I will be a father to them. You and I will raise them together."

Meg regarded him in silence for a moment. He was right. She had been under the impression that although he wanted heirs, he wasn't interested in raising the children. "In that case, I want your word that any differences of opinion we might have as to the upbringing of our children would be discussed and a compromise sought.''

''Agreed.'' He frowned impatiently at the anxiety that remained in her eyes. ''You don't have to look so worried. I'm not going to become a domineering ogre who has to have everything his way.''

''I'm relieved to hear that,'' she admitted, adding honestly, ''I do think it's important for you to want to be a part of the children's lives. I've always believed that two caring parents are better than one.''

''I'm glad you feel that way.'' His jaw relaxed and the uneasiness she'd sensed in him earlier disappeared.

The baby she'd put down a few minutes before woke and started to fuss. As she picked the little girl up, she heard a playful squeal from across the room. The two crawlers had found the blocks and were happily throwing them at one another.

''Hey, you two,'' Zeke said, striding across the room and scooping up the two youngsters, one in each arm. ''You don't throw the blocks at one another. You build with them.'' Seating himself on the floor Indian-fashion, he sat the children down and began to show them how to build a tower.

Almost immediately, one of the babies crawled off to find another toy. The other waited until the tower was about five blocks high, then swung an arm out and knocked it down. As the blocks scattered, he looked at Zeke and squealed happily. ''So that's the game,'' Zeke said with a gentle laugh, and began rebuilding the tower so it could be destroyed again.

Zeke Wilson was definitely a man of surprises, Meg thought as she watched him. Never, in her wildest dreams, had she imagined him spending his time playing with a baby. What really amazed her was how natural he looked down there on the floor. The toddler waddled over to see what the fun was all about and seated himself on Zeke's knee. As if he'd been playing with children all his life, Zeke shifted the older child into a more secure position and started handing him blocks so he could build the towers.

Meg made certain the two sleeping babies were comfortably tucked in, then, seating herself in the rocker, she began to rock the cranky baby she was holding while keeping an eye on the third child on the floor. The only sounds in the room were the steady creaking of her chair, the giggles from the children playing with Zeke and his low, answering laughter.

A wistful smile played across Meg's face. This was the kind of scene she wanted to see in her own living room played out by her husband and their children. For the first time, she honestly began to believe that this marriage between her and Zeke might work.

Suddenly the door opened, and Meg's smile vanished as Rita Gaint entered.

"Hi, Meg," she said without even looking toward the rocking chair. Her attention was riveted on Zeke. "I was helping with the three- and four-year-olds when I heard Zeke was in here." Crossing the room, she came to a halt in front of him. "And I had to pop in and see for myself."

"I'm getting in a little practice," Zeke explained as the toddler suddenly lost interest and wiggled off his lap.

Rita's gaze shifted to Meg. Behind the curiosity on her face, there was a calculating look in her eyes. "I heard you two were getting married."

"I decided it was time I settled down," Zeke replied to the question in Rita's voice.

Returning her attention to him, Rita laughed and shook her head in a way that caused her long red hair to swing sexily. "If I'd known that you were the marrying kind, I would never have gone back to Frank."

Meg heard the invitation in the woman's voice. She saw Zeke's jaw tense slightly and knew he'd heard it, too. For the first time it occurred to Meg that Zeke had lied about his feelings for Rita. Maybe he was in love with her. Maybe when she'd gone back to Frank, Zeke had merely put on a good show of not caring. Meg's stomach knotted. Maybe he settled for marrying her because he thought he couldn't have Rita.

"You and Frank belong together," Zeke said, as if stating a fact that was carved in stone.

Rita's mouth formed a thoughtful pout. "I suppose so," she replied, but there was doubt in her voice.

Meg drew a shaky breath. "Don't you have some three- and four-year-olds who need your attention?" she questioned with a calm she didn't feel.

Rita glanced toward Meg and shrugged. "Guess so," she said. Then turning back to Zeke, she smiled. "See you later." The tone of her voice made it a promise.

Meg watched the door close behind the woman. The comfortable atmosphere of the room had been shattered. She looked at Zeke and wondered what was going on in his mind. A part of her didn't want to know. But she'd never been one to hide from the truth. "Would you rather be marrying Rita?" she asked stiffly.

Looking up from the tower he was building, he met her gaze levelly. "No. Our arrangement suits me just fine."

It occurred to Meg that Rita would want an emotional commitment and Zeke Wilson had made it clear he was determined to avoid the pitfalls of a romantic entanglement. Aloud she said, "I just thought I should ask."

His expression became shuttered as he continued to study her. "That's twice this morning that you've asked me if I really want to marry you. Are you having second thoughts?"

Meg looked down at the sleeping baby in her arms. "No," she replied.

"Just thought *I* should ask," he said, then returned his attention to the babies on the floor.

Chapter Nine

The next two weeks passed, and each day Meg grew increasingly nervous. Zeke came over every evening. But his time with her was spent in a reading lesson or finalizing plans for the wedding. There was no feeling of intimacy in their association.

Two days before the ceremony she began moving her clothes and other personal belongings into his home. As she hung her dresses in the closet, her eyes kept straying to the bed. Thoughts of her wedding night excited her and frightened her at the same time. Anxiously she wondered what kind of lover Zeke would be. It occurred to her that because they weren't romantically involved, the consummation of their marriage might be a fairly perfunctory event. *It doesn't matter how the marriage is consummated,* she told herself sternly, *just so it is*. Pulling her gaze away from the bed, she ordered herself not to think about it....

But that order had been easier to give than to obey. The two days had quickly passed. The wedding was over. She'd tossed her bouquet to the group of unmarried female cousins and one widowed aunt. Zeke had tossed her garter to the unattached males. They'd run the gauntlet of rice-throwing well-wishers and now Zeke was driving her to his farm.

Because it was the middle of the school year and she had to be in her classroom Monday morning, they were going to have to wait until the winter break to go anywhere for a honeymoon.

"I thought everything went well," she said, breaking the uneasy silence that had fallen between them.

"I thought so, too," he replied, keeping his full attention on the road.

"Rev. Howard did a good job," she persisted, trying to keep a conversation going. Her nerves felt too on-edge to deal with another silence.

"Yeah," he agreed.

It was clear he was in no mood for conversation. Giving up, Meg studied the hard line of his jaw. He'd gone through all the motions of being the proper bridegroom, but she'd seen the guardedness in his eyes, and when he'd kissed her at the altar it had felt as close to impersonal as a kiss could get. She couldn't help wondering if he already felt trapped by their marriage.

Dusk was falling as they parked in front of the house. A blue Ford was parked nearby.

"Looks like Jess is still here," Zeke said, noticing the car, too.

Bob Slomner was Zeke's full-time farmhand. Jess Marely worked when Zeke needed extra help. Both had been at the wedding, but Meg had noticed that Jess left the reception early. Obviously he'd gotten the job of taking care of the evening chores.

Gathering up her wedding gown, Meg waited until Zeke came around and opened her door. Trying to keep the dress off the ground she gently eased herself out of the car.

"It's going to be hard for you to walk across this gravel drive in those high heels and holding onto that dress," he said as her heel sunk into the loose pebbles. "I'd better carry you."

Before Meg knew what was happening, he'd lifted her in his arms and was striding toward the porch. A nervous excitement filled her. Shyly she glanced at him. There was only indifference on his face. He could be carrying a sack of grain for all he cares, she thought, and her body stiffened.

Reaching the level of the porch, he set her down and found his keys. Watching him calmly unlocking the door, her anger grew. Here she was practically a nervous wreck worrying about their wedding night and he was showing as little interest in her as he would a piece of furniture. As soon as the door was opened, she stepped inside.

"Thought I was supposed to carry you over the threshold," he said, entering behind her.

She met his cool gaze with equal coolness. "Since this isn't a traditional marriage, I didn't see any reason for us to adhere to tradition."

"You've got a point," he conceded. He was standing with the door open. Glancing back at the blue Ford, he frowned. "I'd better go see if Jess has run into some trouble. You change into something less cumbersome and we'll drive into Kansas City for dinner."

Before Meg could even respond he strode out of the house and was on his way toward the barn.

"Yes, master," she muttered, shoving the door closed. Gathering up her dress, she went up to their bedroom. Entering it, she glared at the big four-poster bed they would share. "I didn't expect him to behave like a man in love, but I did expect him to show some interest in me," she muttered, as she began unfastening her gown.

Hanging the wedding dress in the closet, she glanced toward the clock. It was already nearly six. If they went into Kansas City for dinner it would be eleven-thirty or even midnight before they got back. They'd probably both be too tired to even try to consummate the marriage. She drew a deep breath. That wasn't what she wanted. The fear, mingled with the anticipation of sharing Zeke's bed, had her nerves on a razor's edge. She couldn't bear to prolong the uncertainty of it any longer.

Putting on a pair of jeans and a sweater, she went down to the kitchen. She knew the refrigerator was well stocked. She'd done that herself. She hadn't wanted to have to go grocery shopping over the weekend.

Taking out the makings for a salad, she began washing a head of lettuce.

Entering the kitchen, Zeke frowned at her questioningly. "Though we were going out for dinner."

"It's been a long day and I'm too tired to go all the way into Kansas City. So I decided to fix something here," she replied with forced nonchalance.

"Sounds fine to me. I'm feeling a bit beat myself." Tossing his suit coat onto a chair, he loosened his tie and unfastened the top two buttons of his shirt. "I'll set out the plates."

Meg told herself she should stop tearing lettuce and finish unbuttoning his shirt. But her courage wasn't built up enough yet to try to seduce a man who showed no interest in her.

She put candles on the table to try to make the meal more romantic. But even the soft glow of the candlelight couldn't warm the chill that persisted between them.

"Did Jess have some trouble with the chores?" she asked, trying to break the ice with some conversation.

"No. He just got a late start," Zeke replied. Cutting another bite of meat, he added, "You're a good cook."

"It's hard to ruin a steak and salad," she responded. She'd tried to sound casual, but her voice came out stiff. She saw him frown impatiently before his expression became shuttered. He's already bored with me, she thought. Concentrating on her food, she called herself a fool for thinking this marriage had even the smallest chance of lasting beyond the first night. By the time the meal was over, her stomach was in a knot. The steak and salad were lying inside like a large stone.

"Jess says the weatherman is predicting a storm front will move through sometime tomorrow morning," Zeke said as they cleared the table.

"My mother said she heard someone predict that we'd have our first snowfall in early November," Meg offered, wondering how many newlyweds discussed the weather on their wedding night. *We're probably the first,* she decided.

"I need to check the fence line," Zeke continued in businesslike tones, as he dried the dishes while she washed. "There's a weak spot down by the west pasture. A heavy snow might bring it down."

Hot tears of frustration burned at the back of Meg's eyes. Even in her worst nightmares, this was not how she had imagined her wedding night to be.

"I'll need to get an early start tomorrow morning to get the chores done before the storm hits," Zeke was saying. "Guess I should be getting to bed early."

There was no invitation in his voice. He was simply talking about getting a good night's sleep. Afraid she might cry in front of him, Meg said with schooled indifference, "Why don't you go ahead? I can finish here."

"Maybe I should," he replied and laying aside the dish towel, he left.

Meg's chin trembled as she heard him climbing the stairs. This was not working out the way she had expected. Trying not to think about her disappointment, she finished the dishes. As she walked out into the hall a few minutes later, she heard the shower being turned off. She glanced indecisively up the stairs.

Coming to a halt in front of a mirror, she stared at her image. I'm not bad-looking, she told herself. Gathering up the excess fabric of the sweater, she turned sideways to get a better view of her figure. There was nothing any reasonable man would find unacceptable about it.

Her jaw hardened in a determined line. He wasn't going to ignore her! She was a woman. She had feminine wiles. They might be a little unused, but they were there somewhere and she'd find them and use them.

Going up to their bedroom, she discovered Zeke sitting propped up in bed studying his reading lesson. The blankets covered him only to the waist exposing the wide, muscular expanse of his bare chest. For a moment her courage faltered as she froze in mid-stride. I can do this, she told herself and ordered her legs to move. "I thought I should get to bed early, too," she said fighting to keep her voice casual. During one particularly bad attack of the premarital jitters she had gone into Kansas City and purchased several very sexy negligees. Pausing at the bureau, she chose a white one and slipped into the bathroom.

After a quick shower, she dressed in the lace-and-satin nightie. It was even more revealing than she remembered. *He's your husband. He's supposed to see you in even less,* she chided herself, when a rush of embarrassment caused her to hesitate as she reached for the doorknob.

Forcing a smile onto her face, she stepped into the bedroom. The lamp on the table on Zeke's side of the bed had been turned off. A light snore let her know that he was already asleep.

Her hands balled into fists. She felt totally humiliated. Grabbing her robe out of the closet, she left the room and went downstairs. The November night was cold and she shivered. Pulling on the robe, she went into the living room. There was an afghan on the couch. Taking it, she curled up in a large upholstered chair near the window and stared out at the night. The stars twinkled, but around the moon was a white, hazy halo. A snow moon, her grandfather Delany used to call it.

Wrapping the afghan more securely around herself, she drew a shaky breath. She hadn't expected him to be so totally indifferent to her presence. *I suppose I'm just supposed to wait until the mood strikes him,* she mused acidly.

There was a click of a switch and light filled the room. "There's no reason for you to spend the night huddled down here," an impatient male voice interrupted her solitude. Startled, she glanced toward the interior of the room to find Zeke coming toward her. He was barefooted and bare-chested, wearing only a pair of faded jeans.

With an agitated motion, he combed his hair back from his face with his fingers. "You don't have to worry. I'm not going to molest you."

Pride caused her back to straighten and shoulders to square. "You've made that abundantly clear."

"Then you want to tell me what you are doing down here?" he questioned curtly, coming to a halt in the middle of the room.

Meg glared at him. Anger took control. "Why don't you tell me what's wrong with my body, that it leaves you so cold?" Tossing off the afghan, she stood. Unfastening her robe she dropped it on the chair. "Are my breasts too small? Too large?"

His jaw tensed. "Your breasts are just fine."

"Then my waist isn't slim enough. Or maybe my hips don't suit you," she suggested acidly. "Not that I'm going to try to change anything for you," she informed him with dignity. "I'm just curious."

"There's nothing wrong with your body," he replied in a low growl.

"You could have fooled me," she snapped. "You were so bored with it, you fell asleep." Feeling suddenly very naked, she grabbed up her robe and pulled it back on. A flush began to spread from her neck upward. She couldn't believe she'd been so blatant.

"I've been trying to be considerate of your feelings," he said gruffly. "You've been tense the past couple of weeks. I thought maybe I'd set the date too soon. I figured you needed some time to adjust to being around me.''

"And so you decided to ignore my presence?'' she questioned sarcastically. Her jaw tightened. "Ever since we left the reception you've been trying to avoid me. You've acted like I was an unwanted nuisance you'd foolishly invited into your home.''

He scowled. "The truth is I wasn't certain how to approach you, or even if I should try. There have been moments during the past few days when I thought I saw fear in your eyes. It's a little hard on a man's ego to think that the woman in his bed is only there because she wants a child... that she views their intimacy as something she has to endure to achieve that end.''

"I have been a little nervous lately,'' she admitted, adding defensively, "but it's only natural for a person to be a little apprehensive about a new experience.''

His gaze narrowed. "By new experience, do you mean sharing a bed with a man you've never slept with before or do you mean simply sharing a bed with a man?''

Her jaw tensed. "I told you I was the old-fashioned type.''

The brown of his eyes darkened with purpose as he approached her. Coming to a halt in front of her, he combed a wayward strand of her hair from her cheek with the tip of his finger. "There has been a major misunderstanding, and it's my fault. I'm willing to live up to my end of our bargain, if you still want me to.''

Swallowing down the nervous lump that suddenly filled her throat, Meg met his gaze levelly. "I want you to."

Smiling crookedly, he lifted her into his arms. But as they left the living room, he did not head toward the stairs. Instead he headed toward the front door.

"Where are we going?" she questioned in confusion.

"We're going to start this night off the way it should have been started off the first time," he replied. Opening the door, he carried her out onto the porch.

A brisk wind whipped around them. "It's freezing out here," she protested, curling up more tightly in his arms.

"Had to bring you out so I could carry you in over the threshold," he explained. Placing a light kiss on the tip of her nose, he turned and carried her back inside.

Beneath her palms she could feel how quickly his skin had cooled. He shivered as he kicked the door closed. "With no shoes and no shirt, you could catch pneumonia pulling a stunt like that," she admonished him.

"I plan to let you warm me up," he replied, starting up the stairs.

Nervous excitement swept through her. "I like the sound of that," she admitted.

When they reached the bedroom he stood her on the floor in front of him. Combing his fingers into her hair, he used his thumbs to tilt her chin upward.

"There is no reason to be afraid. What we're going to do is a very natural thing."

"I'm not afraid," she replied. "I'm just a little apprehensive." With an anxious smile she added, "This time it's your turn to teach me."

"I'll do my best," he promised.

He was massaging the taut cords at the back of her neck and she thought at any moment she might begin to purr. "That's all any person can ask of another," she managed to say.

"We'll start with a kiss." He claimed her lips gently at first. When he met no resistance, his claim became more possessive.

She began to feel light-headed. Searching for support, she rested her hands on his chest. The crisp hair and hard musculature beneath her palms sent rivulets of excitement racing through her. Like a child who has just discovered a favorite new toy, her hands moved caressingly upward to his shoulders.

"I can tell you are going to be a very good student," he murmured against her lips as he slowly finished the kiss and lifted his head away.

Chewing on her bottom lip, she smiled self-consciously.

"The next step is to get rid of this robe." Unbelting her robe, he slipped it off her. Tossing it onto the chair, he let his gaze travel over her body. "And now it's time to thoroughly evaluate my earlier assessment."

She frowned at him in confusion.

"You asked me a lot of questions downstairs," he explained, squatting down in front of her. "I want to make certain my answers were accurate."

He raised and lowered his eyebrows in a Groucho Marx fashion and she saw the mischievous gleam in his eyes. She hadn't expected him to exhibit a sense of humor at this particular moment. It had been her impression that men took sex very seriously. But there he was, playfully trying to put her at ease. A bashful smile spread over her face.

Placing a hand on the outside of either of her legs, he began to trail them slowly upward, carrying the negligee with him.

As his hands moved along her calves and then her thighs, a fire ignited within her. The flames were scorching by the time he reached her hips.

"Very nice," he said, straightening to stand in front of her. His hands continued to rest against her skin with the negligee draped over his wrists. His fingers circled her waist, and his smile deepened. "Very, very nice."

Her breath locked in her lungs as his explorations continued upward over her ribcage to her breasts. "Perfect," he said gruffly.

Meeting his dark gaze, she saw desire smoldering in the depths of his eyes. The fire within her flamed hotter. Raising her arms, she let him finish removing the gown. As it joined the robe on the chair, she moved into his embrace.

"You are beautiful," he said, trailing kisses along her shoulder to her neck.

Primitive urges stirred within her and the passion she had seen in his eyes gave her courage to act. "I suppose I should do some inspecting of my own," she said huskily.

The mischievousness returned to his eyes. "Just remember that we men have fragile egos," he said, releasing her.

Her fingers trembling slightly, she reached for the snap on his jeans. As the sturdy columns of his legs were exposed, she swallowed a nervous lump that developed in her throat. "I find it hard to believe there is anything fragile about you," she said as he stepped out of the jeans and she tossed them onto the chair with her robe and gown.

Laughing softly, he lifted her into his arms and carried her to the bed.

As hard as she tried to quell it, apprehension suddenly filled her.

Seeing the fear in her eyes as he laid her down, he kissed her lightly. "Relax," he said soothingly, stroking her gently as he lay down beside her.

"You do have very capable hands," she murmured, feeling her fear fade as his caresses again clouded her mind with desire.

"And you have a very inviting body," he replied huskily.

His touch swept her away to a world of exquisite sensation. She trembled from the fire that filled her and arched against him to invite his possession. Only for a moment was there any pain, then it was forgotten as passion again ruled her senses.

Later as she lay in the warm curve of his arm, he kissed her lightly on the top of the head. "I didn't hurt you, did I?" he questioned with concern.

"No." Lifting her head, she found him watching her guardedly. "You are a very good teacher."

The guardedness disappeared and he smiled. "You're a very good student."

Snuggling back into his arm, she suddenly found herself wondering how many other women he had held the way he was holding her. The question caused a sharp twinge in her abdomen. *It would be stupid to be jealous,* she chided herself curtly. *It wasn't as if they were two people in love. You should simply enjoy the pleasure of his company, but don't get emotionally involved,* she ordered herself. With that thought firmly in mind, she drifted off to sleep.

Chapter Ten

The next morning when she awoke, she was alone. For a moment she felt as if she'd been deserted. He could have at least kissed me goodbye when he left, she thought. Then she scowled at herself. That wasn't rational. She and Zeke weren't some love-struck couple doting on each other's every breath.

After dressing in jeans and a sweater, she went down to the kitchen. The faint odor of bacon was still in the air. Obviously Zeke had made himself breakfast. He'd also cleaned up all his dishes and pans. Meg felt almost like an interloper as she searched for the coffee. She found it difficult to think of this kitchen as being hers now as well as his.

Finding the coffee, she started a fresh pot perking. As the aroma filled the air, she wandered over and looked out the window toward the barn. She saw Bob and Jess tossing hay onto a wagon hooked up to the tractor, but she didn't see Zeke. Memories of their lovemaking came back into her mind and a warmth stirred inside her. She looked harder, trying to spot him. When she couldn't, an unexpected wave of disappointment washed over her. "You're thinking about him too much," she warned herself.

Determined to put him out of her mind, she found her briefcase and pulled out the stack of tests she needed to grade before Monday.

She was halfway through them when Zeke came back to the house. Looking up from the test she had been grading, she frowned when he didn't immediately come into the kitchen. Hearing him out on the back porch kicking off his boots, she scowled at herself for being so impatient for a sight of him. Determinedly she forced herself to return her attention to the test in front of her. But as the door swung open, she looked up quickly.

"Morning," he greeted her in an easy drawl, entering the kitchen in his stocking feet. "Hope I didn't wake you this morning."

"You didn't," she assured him. Not wanting him to guess how anxious she had been to see him, her manner became briskly businesslike. Shoving the papers back in her briefcase, she rose from the table. "What can I fix you for lunch?" She had meant to sound casual. Instead her nervousness gave a terse edge to her words.

His expression became shuttered and the temperature in the room seemed to drop ten degrees. "Didn't mean to interrupt you." His eyes traveled to her briefcase, then back to her. "You go ahead with whatever you were doing. You're not here to wait on me. I'll fix my own lunch as soon as I clean up."

He was gone before Meg could think of something to say. Her manner and voice had made it seem as if he had intruded on some important work she was doing. Angrily she gave herself a mental kick. She didn't want there to be a chill between them. *You set the tone,* she scolded herself. "Then I'll just have to unset it," she muttered and took off after him. He was halfway up the stairs by the time she rushed out into the hall. "Wait!" she called out.

Pausing, he looked down at her. "What do you want?" His tone implied that she was the intruder this time.

For a moment she balked. Then reminding herself that this current rift between them was her fault, she climbed the stairs and came to a halt a step below him. Apologetically she said, "I didn't mean to sound so..." she paused, hunting for the right word.

"Cold?" he suggested dryly.

"Cold," she conceded. "It's just that I'm feeling a little uneasy. I'm not certain where I fit in here." She made a sweeping gesture with her hand to indicate his house. "I'm not certain how I fit into your life."

Impatience showed on his face. "You're my wife," he replied bluntly, as if that should answer all her questions.

"Your wife," she repeated. She liked the sound of that more than she wanted to admit. A self-conscious smile played at the corners of her mouth. "All right. Then as your wife, I feel it would be a very wifely thing to do if I fixed you lunch. So what would you like?"

His jaw softened. "Soup and sandwiches would be fine."

"Soup and sandwiches it is," she replied, and hurried back to the kitchen.

By the time Zeke had showered and come back downstairs, Meg had the meal on the table.

"Looks good," he said, seating himself.

As they began to eat, a silence threatened to descend between them. Too nervous to let that happen, Meg asked, "Did you get the fence repaired?"

Zeke looked at her in surprise. "How did you know about the fence?"

"You mentioned yesterday that you had a fence that needed mending," she explained.

"Guess I did." He looked a little sheepish, and she guessed he was remembering their confrontation the night before. Then the brown of his eyes softened and she knew he was remembering how it ended. "Yeah, we got it repaired," he said. "Jess and Bob will take care of any other chores that need to be done today. I thought it would look sort of peculiar if I didn't want to spend the major portion of the day with my new bride."

"I suppose it would," she agreed. The way he was looking at her was causing a warmth to spread from her toes upward.

He nodded toward her briefcase. "Do you have some work you need to get done this afternoon?"

"It can wait until tomorrow," she replied. Scared by how much she wanted to spend an intimate afternoon with him, she forced herself to remember his very practical reason for marrying her. "Of course we should go over your reading lesson sometime today."

"I was thinking the same thing myself," he said and applied himself to finishing his lunch.

A cold lump formed in Meg's stomach. Obviously she wasn't affecting him the same was he was affecting her. He's had more experience; *it's old hat to him,* she reasoned. *And* she added curtly, *after a while the newness of his lovemaking will wear off and I won't be so anxious to share his bed.* However, at the moment her current level of interest was exceptionally high. Determined not to be too obvious, she forced herself to finish her meal.

As she carried her empty dishes to the sink, Zeke rose and carried his over, as well. But when she turned on the water to wash them, Zeke turned it off.

"I was thinking," he said, moving her hair away from her ear with the tips of his fingers and placing a light kiss on the sensitive skin behind the ear. "My reading books are upstairs by the bed."

"We could go get them," she suggested as he trailed kisses down the taut cord of her neck.

He raised his head and smiled mischievously. "Now that's a very good idea." Lifting her into his arms, he carried her out of the kitchen and up the stairs. "I think the best way to start this afternoon is for me to give you another lesson," he said, kissing the tip of her nose as he stood her on the bedroom floor. "Then you can give me my reading lesson," he continued as he began removing her sweater. "And then you can reward me for being such a good student."

"Sounds like a busy afternoon," she managed, her blood pulsing through her veins in excited anticipation.

On Sunday morning, she again awoke alone.

In the kitchen she again found that he'd fixed himself breakfast and cleaned up his dishes and pans. However, this time he did leave coffee warming in the pot.

"At least today he remembered I was upstairs," she murmured, pouring herself a cup.

She was sitting at the table, nibbling on a piece of toast and correcting tests when he came in. Pausing only long enough to wish her a cursory good morning from across the room, he barely broke stride as he hurried through the kitchen on his way upstairs.

A surge of disappointment washed over her. Grudgingly she admitted that she had expected him to at least give her a quick kiss. *You don't have that kind of marriage,* she reminded herself curtly. *You have a practical arrangement.*

Drawing a sigh, she forced herself to concentrate on the paper in front of her.

When Zeke reappeared twenty minutes later, he was dressed for church. "We'd better be leaving," he said, crossing the room and unplugging the coffeepot.

Again Meg felt a wave of disappointment when he didn't pause to kiss her. *You've got to stop expecting him to behave like a man in love, because he isn't,* she scolded herself.

But she could not fault his behavior when they arrived at church. He came around the truck and opened her door for her, then offered her his arm as they started walking toward the entrance. To any nosy gossip watching, they looked like a happily married, much-in-love couple.

Winter had arrived. The cold had forced those parishioners who normally gathered on the lawn to visit before the service to seek shelter in the sanctuary.

But as they approached the church, Kate came out to meet them. Reaching them, she caught Zeke's arm and brought him and Meg to a halt. "I know this may sound a bit pushy," she said, keeping her voice lowered so that no passing churchgoers could overhear. "But I would like for the two of you to come to Sunday dinner."

The invitation bordered on being a command.

"Is there something wrong?" Meg asked worriedly.

"No." Kate's gaze traveled from her daughter to Zeke. "I just want to assure myself that this marriage of yours is going well."

Meg flushed with embarrassment. "It's going just fine."

"Then you won't mind having dinner with me so I can see for myself," Kate insisted.

Meg was about to tell her mother that there was no reason for them to have dinner with her, when Zeke interrupted. "We'd be pleased to come," he said with a polite smile. "Next to your daughter, you're the best cook I know."

Kate smiled with relief. "I'll join you in church," she said, waving to Mrs. Royd who had just arrived. "I'm going to go say hello to Norma."

As she walked away, Meg turned to Zeke. "I want to apologize for my mother. She has no right to question our marriage like that." Her frown deepened. "I really don't know what's gotten into her. She told me that she liked you."

"It's all right," he assured her. "You and your mother are close. It's only natural she'd be worried about your welfare."

Meg frowned musingly. Zeke Wilson was proving to be a great deal more understanding and patient than she had ever imagined him to be. *It's because he's not emotionally involved,* she reasoned. *To him it's strictly business.*

"Meg. Zeke." A woman's voice interrupted Meg's thoughts. Looking up, Meg saw Rita Gaint coming toward them. She had Frank in tow. "Well, well, if it isn't the happy couple," Rita said cheerfully, as she and Frank came to a halt in front of Meg and Zeke.

"It's freezing out here," Frank interjected angrily before any polite exchanges could be made. "Just say hello, Rita, and let's get inside."

Rita gave Meg and Zeke a quick smile. "Hello," she said as Frank dragged her toward the church.

Just about everyone in Vincent's Gap knew how much Frank hated getting up on Sunday morning. Even worse, he hated putting on a suit and going to church. "I wonder how she got him here this morning?" Meg mused, watching the pair scurry toward the entrance. "From what I hear, it's a challenge to get him here on Easter and Christmas."

"Rita has her ways of getting what she wants," Zeke replied matter-of-factly.

Meg's stomach knotted. *Zeke would know*, she thought. Aloud she said tightly, "It is cold out here. We should be getting inside."

Zeke nodded and they went into the church. They made their way to the pew Meg and Kate always sat in. Kate was there, keeping places for them. "What did Rita want?" she demanded the moment Meg seated herself.

"Just to say hello," Meg replied, attempting to ignore the knot still in her stomach.

Kate gave a disbelieving snort. "She ought to be concentrating on that husband of hers, and leaving you and Zeke alone."

Meg glanced toward Zeke to see if he was looking for Rita, but he was looking at the Sunday bulletin. From the stern expression on his face, she knew he was trying to read it. And he will be reading it in a few months, she judged. He was the very best student she'd ever had. He studied diligently and he was smart. Suddenly she found herself wondering how he would rate her as a pupil. The thought that she might not fair as well as Rita caused the knot in her stomach to tighten. *I am not in competition with her,* she told herself firmly. Still the knot did not go away.

However, Meg's uneasiness about Rita did fade to the background as the service continued. Her mother posed a more immediate problem. There were times in the past when Kate had been less than tactful, and Meg did not want her embarrassing Zeke or alienating him.

As they left the church, she gave her mother a warning look. Kate acknowledged that she'd seen it with a self-righteous shrug.

Meg groaned mentally and prepared herself to be the buffer between her mother and Zeke.

While Meg waited uneasily for the confrontation to begin, Kate talked about the sermon during the ride from the church to her home. Once they were there, she busied herself with putting the meal on the table. But as they sat down, Kate turned her attention to Zeke, and Meg's whole body stiffened with anticipation.

"Are you treating my daughter well?" Kate asked him bluntly.

"He's treating me very well," Meg interjected sharply.

Both Zeke and her mother ignored her. Facing Kate levelly, Zeke said, "I'm doing my best."

"Just see that you continue to do your best, or you'll have me to answer to," Kate warned.

"Yes, ma'am," Zeke replied solemnly.

Kate smiled her approval. "Now eat," she ordered.

Meg looked worriedly at Zeke but he showed no sign of having been offended. As she began passing the food, Kate turned the conversation to local politics and Meg breathed a sigh of relief. Her mother had actually behaved.

But when the meal was over, Kate shooed Zeke into the living room. "You read the Sunday paper," she directed. "Meg can help me with the dishes."

It was obvious Kate wanted a private word with her daughter. Again Meg glanced worriedly toward Zeke and again she saw no hint of offense on his face. She wouldn't have blamed him if he'd been a little angry. If she'd been in his place, she would have been. *I'm a business deal to him,* she reminded herself curtly. *He doesn't care what my mother thinks.* She watched him as he strode out of the room. He'd spent a lifetime not letting anyone get close enough to make him care what they thought.

Pulling her attention away from him, she carried a stack of dishes into the kitchen.

Kate waited until all the dishes had been brought in and she and Meg were washing and drying them, then in worried tones she asked, "Is everything between you and Zeke really all right?"

"Everything is fine," Meg assured her.

A slight flush tinted Kate's cheeks. "Are there any questions you want to ask me?" The flush deepened. "Are you enjoying being married?"

Meg couldn't help smiling at her mother's self-conscious attempt to offer womanly advice about any problems that might have surfaced on her wedding night. "No, I don't have any questions, and I am enjoying being married," she assured her. *Maybe I'm enjoying it too much,* she added to herself.

"I'm glad to hear that." But instead of relief showing on her face, Kate frowned as she continued washing the dishes.

Meg knew that look. "All right, out with it," she ordered. "Something is on your mind and none of us is going to have any peace until it's out."

Letting the dish she had been washing sink back into the water, Kate turned to face her daughter squarely. "There have been a lot of rumors about your wedding."

Meg shrugged. "I know that."

Kate regarded Meg worriedly. "Some people are saying that Zeke married you on the rebound. They're saying that he's still in love with Rita, but because he couldn't have her, he married you."

Meg remembered Zeke's assurance that he and Rita were just friends. She wanted to believe him. "You really don't have to worry about my marriage to Zeke. There is no pretense between us. We both know where we stand," she said with a confidence she didn't feel.

Kate looked a little relieved but not entirely. "I just don't want you getting hurt," she said, giving Meg a tight hug.

I won't be as long as I remember the ground rules for my marriage, Meg told herself.

Zeke came in about the time the two women were finishing. "I've got a few chores I left undone this morning," he said. "Thought I'd better be getting back and attend to them." His manner was indifferent as he directed his full attention to Meg. "If you want to stay and visit with your mother, I can come back for you later."

For a split second her pride almost caused her to tell him to go ahead without her. But catching a glimpse of her mother's watchful eye, she bit back the words. She was in no mood for an afternoon of subtle prying. "I'll come with you. I've still got a stack of papers to grade." Before Kate could protest, Meg was following Zeke to the hall closet.

"I didn't mean to cut your visit with your mother short," Zeke said a few minutes later, as he climbed in behind the wheel of his truck.

"I don't mind," Meg replied honestly. She told herself that she was simply happy to be away from her mother's prying. She refused to admit how much she enjoyed being alone with Zeke, especially when he didn't care if she was there or not.

Pulling away from the house, Zeke asked, "Did you assure your mother that I wasn't brutalizing you?"

Meg glanced toward him. She'd heard the edge in his voice and she caught the momentary flash of anger in his eyes. "You were angry," she said in astonishment.

He shifted his shoulders as if he was suddenly uncomfortable. "Any man would be."

She studied him narrowly. "You are exceptionally good at hiding the way you feel."

"My feelings are nobody's business but my own," he replied grimly.

Meg continued to watch him closely. There was something she needed to know. "My mother wasn't worried about you brutalizing me physically. She was worried about you hurting me emotionally. There are rumors going around that you married me on the rebound...that you are still in love with Rita."

Zeke was stopped at a stop sign. Turning toward her, he met her gaze levelly. "I was never in love with Rita, and I'm not in love with her now. I've already told you that."

Meg searched his face but she could read nothing. "I can't tell if you're telling me the truth or lying."

They were on the main road. Pulling off onto the shoulder, Zeke turned to face her grimly. "I never lie."

Studying the taut line of his jaw, she remembered his proposal. "And you never let anyone get too close," she added.

A mischievous gleam sparkled in his eyes as he sensually ran his finger over her lips. "I thought we got real close."

His touch turned her blood to fire. "That's not what I meant," she said, wishing she had more resistance to him.

He scowled cynically. "There is nothing wrong with being a practical man instead of a weak-minded romantic who thinks his world will be destroyed if he loses the woman he loves."

Meg thought of the laughing little boy in the photo on the mantel and her gaze narrowed on the grim-faced man in front of her. "You're afraid of falling in love. You're afraid of being hurt."

"I prefer to think of myself as a man who doesn't go looking for trouble," he replied dryly. Shifting the truck into gear, he pulled back onto the road.

As silence settled between them, Meg stared out the windshield. She didn't have to worry about Zeke being in love with Rita. He was a man with a strong will, and that will was directed at not falling in love with any woman.

And as long as I keep that firmly in mind and don't go doing anything stupid like falling in love with him, everything will work out fine, she told herself. But the lingering feel of the touch of his finger on her lips taunted her. Excitement stirred inside of her at the thought of being in his arms. *All I'm feeling is a strong physical attraction,* she assured herself curtly. Determinedly she added, *and it's not going to go beyond that.*

Chapter Eleven

On Monday morning, Meg awoke alone once again. Dawn was barely breaking over the horizon. Walking over to the window she looked out toward the barn. A lone figure was striding purposefully toward the pen where forty-two hogs waited to be fed. A sudden urge to go out and help him startled her. She'd never thought of herself as being a farm girl. Besides it was cold out there. Still, the urge remained strong.

"You've got to go teach school," she reminded herself, and forcing her legs to move her away from the window, she made the bed, then dressed.

Later, down in the kitchen, she stood looking out the window over the sink as she took her last sip of coffee. It was time for her to leave and Zeke wasn't anywhere in sight. She didn't like admitting it, but she

had hoped to say goodbye. Grudgingly she realized
that she even hoped for a kiss to send her on her way.
*Good-morning and goodbye kisses belong in a tradi-
tional marriage,* she chided herself. *And the one thing
you and Zeke don't have is a traditional marriage.*

Frowning at herself for trying to get one last glimpse
of him, she left the window. *You're looking for trouble,* she warned herself. Pulling on her coat, she picked
up her briefcase and left.

The morning passed quickly. But during her lunch
break she suddenly found herself thinking of Zeke and
wishing she was there to share lunch with him. *I've got
to stop thinking about him so much,* she ordered herself. *It's too dangerous.* She was not stupid. She knew
there was a strong possibility he would get bored with
her and want out of this marriage. *I've got to keep a
practical view of our arrangement.*

Driving home that afternoon, she tried to feel indifferent toward seeing him. But when she pulled up
and he came out the front door to greet her, her heart
beat a little faster.

"Joan's here," he said, taking her briefcase to carry
it up to the house for her. "She wants to spend
Thanksgiving and Christmas with her children. Since
none of them lives near here, that means she'll be out
of town for better than a month. Normally when she
goes off on one of her trips, I hire someone to come in
and take care of the books until she gets back, then she
checks over the records to make sure everything was
done properly. But she says if you're willing she can

teach you how to do all the bookkeeping that's necessary.''

Meg felt a sudden rush of disappointment that he hadn't come out simply to welcome her home. *You've got to stop reacting to him this way,* she ordered herself. Aloud she said, ''Sure. I'll take care of the books for you.''

His expression became apologetic. ''I know you've got enough work to do with your teaching, but I really appreciate this. I have a feeling Joan is going to want to retire soon and this way you'll have some time to practice and weed out any problems.''

''I honestly don't mind,'' she assured him. That she honestly meant this, shocked her. Balancing her bankbook was not one of her favorite activities. It suddenly dawned on her that she was so willing because it made her feel more like a real part of Zeke's life. Forcing herself to keep a realistic view of the situation, she said aloud, ''It was part of the deal we made.''

''Yeah,'' he replied, with a nonchalant shrug, and opened the front door for her to enter.

An hour and a half later, Meg felt fairly certain she knew what to do with the books. Basically it was a simple matter of record-keeping.

''Just remember to enter every bill and expenditure and mark if it was paid,'' Joan said for about the thirtieth time as she closed the ledger. She was a short woman, a little on the plump side, with gray hair, piercing blue eyes and a brisk business manner. ''I also go over every bill with Zeke before I enter it. He keeps a running total in his head. Don't know how he does it, but he knows every cent he spends and makes.''

"I will," Meg promised. She wasn't surprised that Zeke could keep such good track of his finances. At the rate he was learning to read, she knew he had a very sharp mind.

Joan nodded as she reached into her briefcase and pulled out a couple of three-by-five cards. "Zeke usually signs his own checks." A smile suddenly softened the older woman's features. "He learned to print in school but he never learned to write. When he got his first checkbook, he insisted on learning to sign a proper signature, so I taught him." The seriousness returned to her face. "Anyway, he asked me to pick up a signature card for you. You just sign right here." She indicated a line at the bottom of the card. "That way you'll be able to write checks on the account."

Zeke is certainly going through all the motions of making this a permanent relationship, Meg thought as she nervously scrawled her signature.

"You better try that again," Joan said with an amused twinkle in her eyes, as she pulled a fresh card out of her briefcase.

Looking down at the signature she'd just scrawled, Meg blushed. It was her maiden name.

"Happens all the time with newlyweds," Joan assured her.

Still blushing, Meg wrote *Margaret Wilson* on the fresh card. For the first time she honestly felt like a part of Zeke's life. He was giving her free access to his finances. Obviously he intended this marriage to work.

"I'll get Zeke's signature on the card on my way out," Joan said, closing her briefcase. Her stern, businesslike demeanor suddenly softened noticeably. Smiling warmly at Meg, she said, "I'm so glad he found someone to share his life with. Truth is, I've been real worried that he'd never settle down. I was here when his mom died. That boy doted on her, same as his father did. Can't blame them. Sarah Wilson was a sweet woman."

Meg warned herself she was treading on dangerous ground, but the urge to understand Zeke better was too strong to resist. She wanted to know about the little boy in the picture. "My mother said it was real hard on Zeke and his father when his mother died," she said levelly, trying not to appear as if she was prying.

"Hard? It was devastating." Joan shook her head sadly. "After the funeral, a few of us came back to the house." Joan rose and walked to the window. "We hadn't been here too long when I noticed Zeke was missing. Because he was big for his age, people had a tendency to treat him as if he was older than he really was. But I didn't think he should be left alone, so I went looking for him." She shook her head again. "It took a bit of doing to find him. He was out in the barn, just sobbing his little heart out. I sat on a bale of hay and held him for ages. Then Pete came out and found us. He told Zeke that men didn't cry. He told him to dry those tears and go back up to the house, and that's what Zeke did.''

In Meg's mind's eye she saw the little dark-haired boy walking toward the house, his grief held in check and his shoulders straight. *He did learn early to hide his emotions from the world,* she mused.

"If you ask me, Pete should have done a little crying," Joan continued, an angry frown wrinkling her brow. "He just held all the grief he was feeling inside and let it eat away at him. 'Course he'd always been the kind of man who kept his feelings to himself. Zeke's a lot like him in that respect. But it wasn't right for him to let his own unhappiness ruin any chance Zeke might have had.''

Meg frowned in confusion. "I don't understand.''

Joan was still frowning toward the barn. "When Zeke was fourteen or fifteen, he had his first case of puppy love. He and that Elbert girl from down the road walked around holding hands and sighing at one another for near three months.''

Even though she knew Cheryl Elbert was now a happily married woman with five children, Meg's stomach knotted. *I am not jealous,* she told herself firmly and concentrated on what Joan was saying.

A smile teased the corners of the older woman's mouth. "They made a cute couple." Then the frown returned. "Anyway, like anyone would expect, they had a squabble. I remember it was a warm summer day and Zeke was sitting on the front porch brooding, when I came by to do the books. I told him that I was sure he and Cheryl would patch things up. Pete came out on the porch about then. 'Told the boy he shouldn't let any woman get under his skin,' Pete said. 'Told him it would only get him hurt.' I told Pete I thought he was being too callous, but he said he was only being realistic.''

"And what did Zeke say?" Meg asked, knowing the answer but needing to hear it anyway.

"He didn't say anything," Joan replied. "But there was this look on his face, as if he was taking what his pa said very seriously. Anyway, he didn't make up with Cheryl even though she came around with a home-made cake as a peace offering." Joan shrugged, and turning back toward Meg, she smiled. "From then on he never seemed to get serious about any woman. But I kept hoping. Then he found you. Guess everything turned out all right, after all.''

Meg forced a smile in response. Joan's stories confirmed what she already knew. At least she wouldn't go getting any romantic notions about Zeke learning to care for her. *And if I'm smart, I won't learn to care for him, either,* she added.

Drawing a tired breath, Joan picked up her briefcase. Suddenly remembering the signature card, her manner became businesslike again. "I need to talk to Zeke," she said.

The aroma of roasting chicken was coming from the kitchen. Following it, they entered to find Zeke opening a can of cranberry sauce.

"I admire a man who's good in the kitchen," Joan said with approval, as she pushed the card in front of Zeke. "All those cooking lessons Barbara gave you have sure paid off.'' Flushing as she realized that she'd mentioned another of Zeke's old girlfriends, Joan stuffed the card in her briefcase as soon as Zeke has scribbled his signature on it, mumbled something about turning the card in the next day, quickly wished Meg and Zeke a good evening and left.

Meg knew who Joan had meant when she said Barbara. It had to be Barbara Lyons, now Barbara Bradley, the home-economics teacher at the high school. Barbara and Zeke had dated a couple of years ago. Barbara had been blatant about her intention of snaring Zeke, but he'd avoided the trap. After a few months she'd admitted defeat and turned to more easily captured game.

Watching him, Meg was tempted to ask if he chose all of his women for the skills they could teach him. But Rita Gaint's image came into her mind and the question died a quick death. As far as Meg knew Rita's talents lay mainly in the bedroom, and she didn't want to hear Zeke's confirmation on that score.

Although she had her doubts about the longevity of their marriage, she had to admit that Zeke seemed determined that it would work. If he thought they couldn't survive together he surely wouldn't have opened his finances to her. And even though she knew it was dangerous to care, she did want this marriage to survive. She hated admitting it, but just being in the same room with Zeke made her feel good.

Determined to let him know that she was willing to do what she could to keep their union stable, she said, "I was thinking that tomorrow I would go by the bank and close out my account and transfer the money into your...our account. I'll also put your name on my savings account.''

He glanced toward her as if he was surprised she would even consider those actions. "There's no reason to do that. You keep your account. Use the money you earn for whatever you like. You're my wife, so you'll use my account for day-to-day living expenses. I had your name put on it because I thought it would be ridiculous for you to have to come to me every time you need money for groceries or a new dress.''

Meg would like to have thought that he was being generous to a fault. But she felt as if he had shut her out. This was his way of keeping the lines between them clearly drawn. *And he probably has his doubts about this marriage lasting, too,* she added. Keeping their money separate would make it easier if they did split. "If that's the way you want it,'' she said with schooled indifference. Determined not to care, she asked, "What can I do to help?''

For the next hour she kept busy, fixing the salad, setting the table and browsing through the newspaper. But as hard as she tried she could not stop the pictures of the grief-stricken little boy or the hurt adolescent from flooding her mind. She found herself covertly glancing at the man he'd become and wondering if the barrier he had built around his emotions would ever fall. Even as he sat relaxed, reading the paper, there was a determined set to his jaw that caused her to believe that barrier was as sturdy as the Rock of Gibraltar and nothing was ever going to penetrate it. *And you'd better never forget that,* she warned herself.

"Have I suddenly grown an eye in the middle of my forehead?" he questioned dryly as they sat down at the table to eat.

Meg glanced at him questioningly. "What?"

"You've been watching me all evening," he elaborated.

Meg started to deny the accusation, but stopped herself. The temptation to find out just how sturdy his barriers were was too strong to resist. "Joan was telling me a little about your youth," she said slowly.

The defiant look she remembered from fifth grade came over his face. "Joan exaggerates."

Meg's gaze rested momentarily on the taut line of his jaw, then shifted to his cold, dark eyes that warned her she was trespassing where she wasn't allowed. *Those barriers of his must be made of steel,* she decided. Turning away from him, she served herself some chicken. But her attempt to pry had caused a tension to settle over the table. She tried to concentrate on her dinner, but the silence between them was deafening. The food she swallowed felt like a hard rock in her stomach. She didn't want the evening to go on like this. "How was your day?" she asked levelly, attempting to defuse the atmosphere.

"Fine," he replied taciturnly.

Meg frowned as silence once again descended between them. Well, he might enjoy living in a shell, but that didn't mean she did. "My day went fairly well, too," she said in a conversational tone. "Except for

the fight between Billy Cole and Jonathan Volar.''
Between bites she related the event.

Zeke finished and sat frowning at her with a shuttered look on his face.

"I'm sorry if I'm boring you," she said. "But I'm
used to talking about my day over dinner. It helps me
get rid of the tension spending several hours with an
active group of teenagers can cause." When he didn't
say anything, she continued coolly, "You don't have
to listen."

"Actually I was enjoying listening," he admitted.

Meg breathed a sigh of relief as the tension in the air
began to disperse.

During the next couple of weeks they settled into a
mutually agreeable routine. Most mornings Zeke was
already out working when Meg rose and left for work.
But he was generally at the house when she arrived
home in the late afternoon. They cooked dinner together and during the meal she talked about her day.
After a while, Zeke began to contribute information
about his day.

In a way it had been easier when he was taciturn,
Meg thought one evening. She was listening to him tell
her about having to go into town twice to find the right
piece for a tractor and found herself feeling his frustration as vividly as if it was her own. *You're supposed to be maintaining an emotional distance,* she
chided herself, then quickly added, *I'm only feeling
what a friend might feel for another friend.* But down

deep she knew that was a lie; she was quickly getting ensnared by the man.

Thanksgiving came. Meg fixed a big meal and invited several members of both families to come.

She would have liked to skip inviting her Aunt Nola but that was impossible. Aunt Nola was a widow with three grown children who lived too far away to make it home for this short holiday. She was in her midfifties, large boned with a domineering air. For the past five years she'd always been invited to join Kate and Meg for Thanksgiving. Meg couldn't ignore her and leave the woman to spend the holiday alone. The problem was Aunt Nola always spoke what was on her mind, and most of the time this involved insulting someone present or maligning someone who was absent. Trying to stop her or keep her quiet was like trying to stop a Sherman tank with a BB gun.

Maybe this year would be different, Meg prayed silently as their guests began to arrive.

But her prayer wasn't answered.

Nola entered like a woman with a purpose. Handing her coat to Zeke with barely a nod of recognition, she turned her full attention to Meg. "Have you heard the news?" she demanded, her voice loud enough to carry into the living room where those who had already arrived were gathered.

"News?" Meg questioned, quickly going over in her mind all the latest gossip that could possible embarrass anyone present. As far as she knew, there wasn't any.

"About Neil Talmage," Nola gushed. "He and that Marlow girl are getting married in Houston in early January. *And* the Talmages have chartered a private plane to fly all their friends and relatives to the wedding. *Not only that*, they've reserved an entire floor in one of the best hotels in Houston to house everyone." Nola glanced around her disparagingly. Bending her head close to Meg's she lowered her voice somewhat, but kept it loud enough for Zeke to hear. "I really can't believe you gave up all that for *this*."

"I'm really very happy here," Meg said firmly, an apology in her eyes as she looked past Nola to Zeke.

He was showing no reaction to what Nola had said, but his Uncle Walter who had arrived just behind Nola looked ready for a fight. He was an elderly man, who'd outlived his wife and two of his three children. His slender frame stiffened for battle. "I'm right surprised Zeke here was willing to give up his whole bevy of pretty women and settle for one," he countered.

Nola rewarded him with a snort and stalked off into the living room.

Walter's face suddenly became apologetic. "I'm sorry, Meg," he said. "I shouldn't have said that. You and Zeke make a fine couple."

"It's all right," Meg assured him. His words had hurt, but she couldn't hold them against him. He'd been coming to his nephew's defense. "Aunt Nola has a knack for bringing out the worst in people." Turning to Zeke, she said, "She had no right to say what she said. I'm sorry."

He shrugged as if he'd barely noticed Nola's jab. Turning to Walter he said, "I've been thinking of buying a new tractor and I'd like your opinion." Taking his uncle by the arm, he gently guided him toward the den.

"I'm really sorry, Meg," Walter apologized again over his shoulder one last time. "I didn't mean it."

Meg gave him an encouraging smile and headed toward the living room. She wanted to make certain Nola hadn't started any fistfights in there.

But now that Nola had delivered her cutting blow, she seemed to have settled down and was talking pleasantly with Kate. Meg gave her mother a look that said "keep Nola under control" and went into the kitchen to check on the turkey. But as hard as she tried not to let it bother her, Walter's crack about Zeke's bevy of women friends taunted her.

Other than that, the day went well. Walter had his temper under control by the time Zeke brought him in to join the others, and Meg noticed Kate giving Nola a sharp kick in the ankles when Nola started to rise and move toward Zeke. Immediately Nola reseated herself and kept a distance between herself and Zeke for the remainder of the afternoon.

It was nearly ten that night, by the time the guests were gone and the kitchen was cleaned up.

"I'm going to take a hot shower," Meg announced as she handed Zeke the last pan to dry.

In the bedroom she stood for a long moment in front of the bureau. "You really let Uncle Walter's jab get to you, didn't you?" she chided the image in the mirror. All afternoon she'd found herself wondering if Zeke missed the variety he was used to. Opening her drawer she pulled out the sexiest negligee she could find.

When she stepped out of the bathroom a little while later, she discovered Zeke standing by the window staring out at the night. He was still dressed in his slacks and shirt.

His expression was grim when he turned toward her. "Do you regret giving up all that Talmage could have given you?" he asked. "All the servants? The luxuries?"

So her Aunt Nola's jab had gotten to him. "No," she answered honestly. "I told you it would never have worked."

"You told me that you didn't love him," he replied coolly. "But you married me and you didn't love me and you've made this marriage work."

Pride wouldn't let her admit to him that his touch turned her body to fire while Neil's had left her cold. It made her sound too wanton. "Neil wanted a wife who was in love with him. Marriage to him would have required too much pretending."

"And with us there is no pretense," he finished dryly.

"Yes," she replied. She caught the hint of impatience in his voice and it puzzled her. Then the ugly truth dawned on her. His uncle's words must have struck a deep cord within him. He was getting bored with her already. Her stomach knotted. She told herself the pain she was feeling was only because she hadn't gotten pregnant. But she wouldn't hold him to an arrangement he didn't want. "Are you regretting having tied yourself to one woman?" she heard herself asking with surprising calm.

For a long moment he regarded her in silence. Drawing a deep breath, he let his gaze travel over her. The brown of his eyes darkened. "Not when you're standing there looking like that," he said.

He moved toward her.

Even before he touched her, her blood was rushing wildly through her veins. At least for tonight he still wanted her. She told herself she was glad because it would give her one more opportunity to have a baby. But as he took her into his arms, she could think of nothing except the warmth and excitement she found in his embrace.

The next morning, however, his noncommittal response taunted her. Her pride again insisted that she give him a way out of the marriage if that was what he wanted. But as she practiced facing him and reacting coolly to his admission that he'd discovered that marriage wasn't for him, a hard lump formed in her throat. Curtly she assured herself that this was due only to regret for the child she might never have.

By the time he came in for lunch, she was ready to face him. She had planned to wait until she placed the meal on the table and they were sitting eating. But her nerves weren't that strong. She waited until he'd washed up at the kitchen sink and was toweling his hands dry, then said with practiced calm, "I want you to understand that I would never hold you to a marriage you don't want."

He raised a cynical eyebrow. "Is this going to lead to a request by you for a divorce? Have you decided that being a farmer's wife isn't what you want? If so, just say it. Don't beat around the bush."

His snide manner caused her jaw to harden defensively. "I wasn't talking about me. I was talking about you. You were very noncommittal last night." A stiffness entered her voice as she forced herself to continue. "I know a man like you is used to variety. Being stuck with one woman can get boring."

A self-conscious smile curled one corner of his mouth. "My reputation is exaggerated." He moved closer to her and placing a finger under her chin, tilted her face upward. "And you do not bore me."

Meeting his gaze, she saw the desire in the dark depths of his eyes and an answering flame sparked in hers. The temptation to stop now and leave the rest of what she had planned to say unsaid was strong. Still she forced herself to continue. "But if I should begin to bore you and you decide you want your freedom, I want you to tell me," she insisted.

"I will tell you," he agreed. A coolness entered his eyes as he added, "And you will tell me if you decide you should want your freedom. We agreed there would be no pretense between us."

"No pretense," she confirmed, remembering his cynical proposal.

The warmth returned to his eyes. "I seem to remember another condition of our marriage." Leaning forward he kissed her very slowly. "And I wouldn't want to be accused of not upholding my part of the bargain."

His hands moved possessively along the curves of her body and Meg saw the desire in his eyes. Immediately her body responded. *This weakness could prove to be destructive,* she warned herself, but rational thought vanished as he kissed the sensitive cord of her neck. "That would be terrible," she agreed huskily.

Reaching toward the stove, he turned off the flame under the soup. "Lunch can wait." Slipping an arm around her waist, he guided her toward the hall.

"Lunch can wait," she agreed, wishing she didn't crave his touch so strongly. But she found that she didn't have the will to fight this hunger he so easily awakened.

Chapter Twelve

December came and Meg began to make plans for Christmas. She had already bought the majority of the gifts for her family, but she had no idea what to get Zeke.

"However," she mused to herself one evening, "a more immediate question is where will we put the Christmas tree." She was standing in the middle of the living room mentally rearranging the furniture, trying to decide where the tree would look best.

After much thought, she concluded that by the window would be the perfect spot. But as she started to move the furniture, she stopped. "I really should ask Zeke first," she muttered, straightening and releasing the arm of the chair she was about to push into a far corner. "After all it is his house."

"*Our* house," a male voice corrected from behind her.

Startled, she jerked around. "I thought you were studying."

"I needed a break," he replied. "Thought I would come and see what you are up to." He was watching her grimly. "And this is as much your house as it is mine."

Meg wanted to believe that. But she was afraid to start thinking in terms of theirs and ours. She was afraid this might lead to more dangerous thoughts. "I was trying to decide where to put the Christmas tree," she said, shifting the conversation to more neutral ground.

He shrugged. "Put it wherever you like."

"I thought in front of the window would be nice," she said uncertainly. She didn't like having the decision dumped entirely on her shoulders. But even more, she wanted to please him. "Where do you usually put it?"

He shifted uneasily. "Haven't had a Christmas tree since..." he paused and his expression became stoic. "Since I was a kid," he finished.

Intuitively Meg knew what he had avoided saying. "Since your mother died," she filled in, then flushed when she realized she'd spoken aloud.

"Since my mother died," he confirmed coolly. Shrugging as if it made no difference, he added, "My dad and I never seemed to have the time."

She wanted to ask about his mother. The temptation to get beyond the barrier he'd built around himself was so strong she could taste it. But she remembered the last time she'd tried. "Do you still have a stand or any ornaments?" she asked instead.

"I think there's a box in the attic." His jaw tensed, as if the thought bothered him. Then with another shrug as if he was trying to rid himself of an unpleasant thought, he said, "Might as well go check."

Meg started to tell him it wasn't necessary to go find the box this very minute, but he was already on his way out of the room. Quickly she followed.

"Careful," Zeke cautioned over his shoulder as he climbed the pull-down ladder. "Give me a second to find the light."

Meg watched him disappear into the darkness above. As she mounted the ladder she heard a click, and a light bulb attached to the rafters just above the ladder came on.

Dust stirred as Zeke shifted boxes. It was a high-ceilinged attic, with room for an adult to stand straight in the center. Rough flooring had been put in. Old furniture, boxes and trunks filled the majority of the space.

"Here it is," Zeke announced, pulling a dust-coated box out of a dark corner and sending an even thicker cloud of dust into the air as he wiped it off.

Meg backed down the ladder and waited in the hall for him to carry the box down.

"Looks like it's still pretty much intact," he said, as he joined her in the hall. Continuing past her, he carried the box downstairs to the living room.

Setting it on the floor in front of the fireplace, he opened it. Lifting out a string of the large, old-fashioned bulbs, he frowned. "We'll have to get new lights. These are too old and the wiring probably isn't safe."

Meg nodded. She was watching him. There was a tenseness in the line of his jaw that belied his casual tone.

Putting aside the lights, he picked up the center piece of the metal tree stand. "This should probably be replaced, too." But he really wasn't paying a lot of attention to it, Meg noticed, as he set it aside without a second glance. His attention was focused instead on a smaller box that filled half of the larger box. Lifting it out, he shoved the larger box aside. Opening the smaller box, he lifted out a blue carton.

Meg saw his jaw twitch as if he was fighting to keep it still. There was a haunted look in his eyes. He was seated Indian-fashion beside the box, but she had remained standing. From her vantage point she could see several tissue-wrapped objects inside.

"I remember these," he said quietly, as he began to unwrap them and place them on the coffee table. "They were my mother's favorites."

"They're beautiful," she said, as he laid the multi-colored ornaments in a row. Some were long and oval, others more rounded. The rounded ones had an indentation in one side filled with a kaleidoscope of color and sparkles.

"I don't know where they came from." Zeke was frowning introspectively and Meg knew he was talking more to himself than to her. "I think maybe my mother's parents gave them to her the first year she and my dad were married." He shrugged. "It was something like that, anyway." His jaw suddenly tensed even tighter.

Meg felt her heart catch in her throat as she saw the wistfulness that suddenly shone in his eyes. Silently she watched as he finished unwrapping the ornament he was holding. It was blue and round. It was medium in size and plainer than the others.

"This was mine," he said stiffly. "My mother told me she bought it the first Christmas after I was born and I always helped her put it on the tree."

Meg's jaw trembled at the pain she saw on his face. In one stride she reached him and sank to her knees beside him. "We don't have to use any of these," she said softly, gently touching the taut line of his jaw.

He stiffened and his expression became shuttered. As if he was suddenly anxious to be rid of it, he placed the blue ball on the table with the others. Rising, he looked down at her. "You may do what you wish. It makes no difference to me."

Rising also, she faced him levelly. "It's not a sin to be sentimental."

"Doesn't serve any useful purpose, either," he returned curtly. Raking an agitated hand through his hair, he added, "It's getting late. I've got to get back to my lesson."

Watching his departing back, Meg sighed. This house would never be *their house*. Zeke was much too determined never to let anyone get close to him again.

Very carefully she rewrapped the ornaments.

* * *

During the next couple of days Meg bought a new stand, new lights and new ornaments. Zeke did volunteer to go with her when she went to find the tree. The weathermen were predicting snow for the weekend, so they went on Wednesday evening.

On the way, they picked up Kate so she could purchase her tree, too. While they didn't have to trudge through any snow, it was cold and damp.

"I can't believe it took an hour to pick out a couple of trees," Zeke said with a shake of his head as he and Meg drove home. They had stayed long enough at Kate's house to help her get her tree set up in its stand and now it was nearly nine.

"A Christmas tree has to be just right," she replied with the authority of one who has purchased trees in the past.

Zeke frowned. "A tree's a tree."

And a woman is a woman. The thought flashed through Meg's mind, bringing a sharp jab of pain. Covertly she glanced toward him and found herself wishing she wasn't simply a practical solution to his problems. *Thoughts like that will only lead to trouble,* she scolded herself curtly.

By the time they got back to the farm and set their tree in its stand, it was nearly ten.

As soon as Meg was satisfied that the tree was straight and positioned where she wanted it, Zeke muttered something about having a headache and went to bed.

Meg's gaze shifted from the Christmas tree to the picture on the mantel. That laughing little boy was lost forever, she conceded tiredly. Again she felt a sharp jab of pain. Ignoring it she, too, went up to bed.

Zeke was already asleep by the time she climbed out of her shower. Trying not to disturb him, she slipped into bed and went to sleep.

The next morning, the ringing of her alarm clock was accompanied by a low male groan. For a moment the sound didn't entirely register in her sleep-fogged mind. Then her eyes shot open. Zeke was still in bed.

Turning over, she saw him easing himself into a sitting position. Reaching toward him, she touched his back to get his attention. "Are you all right?" The question was unnecessary. His skin felt scorching under her touch. "You're sick," she said in the next breath.

"Just a touch of a cold or something," he muttered, starting to stand, then sinking back to a sitting position on the side of the bed.

Moving swiftly, Meg climbed out of her side of the bed and hurried around to stand in front of him. Pressing her hand against his forehead, the frown on her face deepened. "You've got a fever."

"I've also got work to do," he muttered, again starting to lever himself into a standing position.

Meg placed a hand on each of his shoulders and shoved him back down. "You are staying in bed. Bob can take care of the chores on his own today," she said firmly, continuing to resist his efforts to rise.

"The corral near the barn needs mending. I brought some cattle in from the back pasture for market. Right now they're in a corral that's not sheltered. They've got to be moved before the snow hits," he growled.

"Bob can mend it," she insisted.

He scowled up at her. "It's a two-man job."

Meg saw the glazed look in his eyes. He was really sick. She couldn't let him go outside. "Then I'll call Jess and see if he can come today."

He shivered. "Maybe I will stay in bed for a while," he muttered. Lying back down, he pulled the covers up tight around himself. "You'd better call Jess now."

Using the phone on the bedside table, Meg dialed the number Zeke gave her.

"Well?" Zeke asked, when she hung up a few minutes later.

"He can't come this morning. He's working at the Edwards' place. But he will be here this afternoon," she replied.

"That should give them time," Zeke muttered. Suddenly throwing off the covers, he again forced himself into a sitting position.

"Where do you think you are going?" she demanded, preparing to push him back into the bed.

"I'm going to use the bathroom and then get an extra blanket," he growled. "It's freezing in here."

Meg frowned worriedly. It wasn't freezing. He was having chills. "I can get you the extra blanket."

"No reason for you to wait on me," he said gruffly, as he headed for the bathroom. "I'm used to taking care of myself."

"I don't mind," she replied, already moving toward the hall closet. After finding a blanket, she waited anxiously by the bed for him to return. When he did, she tucked him in and covered him.

He muttered a "thank you" and pulled the covers up to his chin as he closed his eyes.

Meg stood looking down at him. Lying there he looked so vulnerable. She had the most incredible urge to protect him. Smoothing a lock of wayward hair from his forehead, she said softly, "I'm going to call the school and tell them I won't be coming in today."

His eyes opened and he looked up at her as if she was crazy. "There's no reason for you to waste your day hanging around here. I'm not used to people hovering over me."

Meg's back stiffened at the rejection in his voice. "I just thought I should volunteer," she said tightly.

He frowned. "I didn't mean that the way it sounded," he apologized gruffly. "I've always taken care of myself and it would be ridiculous for you to stick around and watch me sleep."

He's never needed anyone before and he's determined not to need anyone now, she thought dryly. Aloud she said, with schooled indifference, "Whatever makes you happy." In her best teacher's voice, she added, "I'll bring you some orange juice and a couple of aspirins. Or would you prefer water?"

"Orange juice sounds fine," he replied.

When she brought him the juice and the aspirin, he took it. As he handed her back the glass, with a gruff self-consciousness that told her he hated asking anyone to do anything for him, he said, "Would you mind telling Bob I won't be out this morning? And tell him that Jess is coming this afternoon to help with the corral."

"I will," she replied, hating the way she still wanted to stay and take care of him even though he didn't want her there.

Thanking her again, he turned over and went to sleep.

Trying not to think about him, Meg dressed. After going out to the barn and giving Zeke's messages to Bob, she came back in and ate breakfast. But before she left she couldn't stop herself from going back upstairs to check on Zeke one last time. He was sound asleep.

"He's right," she told herself as she drove to work. "He doesn't need you watching over him." Her jaw tensed. "Even more to the point, he doesn't *want* you watching over him."

Still she couldn't stop herself from worrying about him.

The weather changed around midday. Clouds moved in and it began to snow. By the time school was dismissed, there were two inches on the ground.

Arriving back at the farm, Meg went immediately up to the bedroom. She'd ordered herself not to. But as she'd entered the house, she couldn't stop herself.

Entering the room, she frowned. Zeke wasn't in bed. She glanced toward the bathroom. The door was open. He wasn't in there, either.

Maybe he got bored and went down to watch some television, she thought, turning and heading back downstairs.

She looked in every room. He wasn't in the house. And his boots and coat were missing from the back porch.

The snow was coming down harder. Obviously the storm that was supposed to hit on the weekend had come early. *And* Zeke was out in it!

"Men!" Meg huffed. "Zeke, in particular! You'd think he'd know better." She cursed under her breath, as she pulled her coat back on and left the house.

She found him in the barn sitting on a bale of hay, holding his head in his hands.

"What in blazes are you doing out here?" she demanded, coming to a halt in front of him. "You were supposed to spend the day in bed."

"Jess called and said he couldn't make it. The storm was moving in, and he had a hole he had to patch in his roof before it hit. So I came out to help Bob with the corral," he explained gruffly, without looking up at her.

"And where is Bob?" she demanded, looking around for the farmhand.

"As soon as we got the corral mended, I sent him home to take care of his own stock," Zeke replied, continuing to hold his head in his hands.

Meg wanted to shake him in anger and hold him protectively, both at the same time. "And then you got so sick, you couldn't get yourself back to the house."

Lifting his head, he stared up at her angrily. "I got a little dizzy so I sat down for a minute," he corrected.

Meg shivered against the cold. Even in the protected barn, it was bitterly frigid. "You're going to freeze if you stay out here any longer. Come on, I'll help you back to the house."

"Can't go in yet." His expression one of grim determination, he rose. "I've got cattle to move."

"You what!" Meg grabbed his arm. "You are in no condition to be herding cattle."

He frowned at her in annoyance. "The corral by the barn offers them more shelter. It has a good windbreak and a lean-to." Shrugging off her hold, he started toward the door.

"You're serious!" She stared at his departing back in disbelief. "You're out of your mind!" Trotting after him, she grabbed his arm again and brought him to a halt. "You could get dizzy, collapse and get trampled."

He scowled at her impatiently. "I don't feel good enough to argue with you. Now leave me alone, so I can get my work done."

"You don't have the sense God gave a mule, but you have the stubbornness," she retorted.

"If you're finished with your insults, I've got work to do," he returned, jerking free from her hold and heading toward a far corral.

"Damn!" she muttered under her breath. Panic mingled with frustration. She'd seen the glazed look in his eyes. He was sick and he needed to be in bed. She jogged to catch up with him.

He glanced down at her irritably. "I'll come inside in a few minutes."

She regarded him coolly. "I'm going to help."

Halting abruptly, he stared down at her. "You don't know the first thing about how to move cattle."

"I'm a fast learner," she replied, and stalked off in the direction he had been heading.

Stopping at the gate of the corral housing the cattle he wanted to move, Zeke again frowned down at her. "I really don't need any help. The gate to the corral by the barn is open. When I open the gate of this corral, I'll hold it across this area." He motioned to the pathway along which they had come. It was about twenty feet wide and lined on both sides by fences. "The cattle won't have any place else to go except to the corral by the barn."

"Fine, then I'll just watch," she said, refusing to leave.

Shrugging, he began unfastening the gate. "Get behind me and stay there," he ordered as he swung the wide wooden barrier open.

But the cattle were all huddled together, fighting the cold. They didn't pay any attention to the open gate.

Meg shifted impatiently. The snow was coming down harder. Zeke couldn't stay out here much longer. He shouldn't be out here in the first place, she fumed. Easing around him, she stared toward the interior of the corral.

"Where the devil do you think you're going?" he demanded, letting go of the gate and capturing her arm.

"It looks to me like they need a little prodding," she answered curtly.

"I'll move them," he growled. "You hold the gate." He shoved a metal-tipped rod into her hand. "If any of them comes your way, give it a little jolt with that."

Meg looked down at the cattle prod. "Won't you be needing it?"

"Never have liked those things," he replied, already heading toward the cattle. Taking off his Stetson, he began hitting the cattle on the rump with it as he yelled at them to get moving.

Meg watched the snow landing on his bare head and her anxiousness grew even more. "Move!" she snarled at a cow that paused to look at her. Immediately the animal backed away and turned toward the barn.

As the last cow came out of the corral and headed toward the barn she swung the gate closed, then trotted to catch up with Zeke.

"I just have to cut the wires on a couple of those bales of hay," he said, motioning toward the feed already waiting in the corral. Running a hand through his snow-wetted hair, he put his hat back on.

He's going to catch pneumonia and end up in the hospital, Meg thought frantically. Impatiently she waited by the gate. When he returned to where she was standing, she glared up at him. "Now you are going inside and staying there," she said in a tone that held no room for compromise.

The hint of a smile played at the corners of his mouth. "I never argue with a woman holding a cattle prod."

Meg didn't smile. She was too worried.

When they reached the house, she sent him upstairs to bed while she heated up some soup.

He was stepping out of the shower when she carried the soup upstairs. "Thought a hot shower might warm me up," he said, shivering visibly. "But it didn't help." Staggering over to the bed, he crawled under the covers.

Meg handed him the cup of soup, then felt his forehead. "You're burning up," she announced tersely. "I'm calling the doctor."

"No reason for that," he growled. "I've felt worse than this and seen it through alone."

"You're just lucky Ida Crammer didn't come in here to clean one Thursday and find you dead," she returned dryly. Stalking out of the room, she used the hall phone downstairs to call the doctor. Zeke had looked deathly pale and glassy-eyed. She was scared so badly her hands were shaking. But she didn't want him to see.

"Can't remember ever making a house call for Zeke," Dr. Evans said jovially, as he entered the house and accompanied Meg up the stairs. "Usually I only see him when he needs stitches, and then he comes in and bleeds all over my office."

Meg forced a smile, but it didn't reach her eyes. She was too worried. Leaving the doctor to examine Zeke, she went down to the kitchen and paced. The moment she heard footsteps on the stairs, she hurried out into the hall.

"Now don't you fret," Dr. Evans told her. "Zeke has the constitution of an ox and his lungs sound clear. He's just got a touch of the flu."

"It looks like more than a touch," Meg said.

"All right, he's got a full-blown case," the doctor admitted, patting her hand. "But as long as he stays in bed and gets plenty of rest, he'll be fine."

Determination glittered in her eyes, as her gaze traveled up the stairs. "I'll see that he does."

"I was sure you would." Dr. Evans gave her a fatherly smile. "Give him some aspirin to bring down his temperature and make certain he has all the liquids he wants."

Meg nodded and thanked him. As soon as the doctor was gone, she went up to Zeke's room. He was already asleep again.

All that night she slept restlessly, waking to every sound Zeke made. Around two he awoke complaining of a monstrous headache. She gave him more aspirin and spent the next hour fixing cold compresses for his forehead.

When her radio alarm clicked on the next morning, she quickly shut it off. Turning back toward Zeke, her eyes rested on his rugged features. Even in sleep there were pain lines across his brow and around his eyes.

She gently touched his cheek. The fever was down a little. A lump of fear formed in her throat as she wondered how many times he'd lain in his bed, sick

with the flu or a cold and no one to watch over him.
Her chin trembled, and the urge to wrap her arms
around him and tell him that he never needed to be
alone again was strong.

Afraid of how she was feeling, she left the bed and
went down to the kitchen. Tears of frustration burned
at the back of her eyes. She didn't want to care so
much. It was dangerous.

As she set up the coffeepot, she considered calling
her mother and having Kate come out and watch over
Zeke during the day. But when she finally picked up
the phone, it was the school she dialed.

Hanging up a few minutes later, she leaned against
the wall in the hall and closed her eyes. Shakily she
admitted to herself that she wanted to be the one who
took care of Zeke. Her chin trembled and she forced
herself to face the full truth. She'd fallen in love with
him. She wanted to be there for him whenever he
needed her. A bittersweet smile curled her lips. The
problem was Zeke was determined to never need her
or anyone.

Calling herself a fool, she picked up the phone and
dialed Bob's number. After talking with him, she went
back upstairs and dressed in a pair of jeans and a
sweater. She had just finished brushing her hair when
Zeke awoke.

"They changed the dress code for school?" he
asked.

"I called in and told them I was taking a sick-leave
day," she replied, watching him in the mirror. She
wasn't ready to face him directly yet this morning. Her

mind was still reeling from her realization of how much she cared for him, and she didn't want him reading it in her eyes.

He frowned. "There was no reason for you to do that."

"I'm your wife. It's my duty to look after you," she replied levelly. The memory of finding him sitting in the barn, cold and sick, assailed her. "You certainly don't do a very good job of looking after yourself," she added tightly.

He rewarded this observation with an impatient scowl. "You being my nursemaid was never in our agreement. I am perfectly capable of taking care of myself."

His words cut like a knife. He didn't want her there. He didn't want her taking care of him. Again she called herself stupid and foolish. Her shoulders squared with pride, as she turned to face him. "I am here because I refuse to be widowed during my second month of marriage. It would make me look like a totally inadequate wife." Without waiting for a response, she stalked out of the room.

Down in the kitchen she stood rigid, her hands clenched into fists. A tear trickled down her cheek. Angrily she brushed it away. She'd known the rules when she agreed to this marriage. She was the one who had broken them by falling in love. But she wasn't going to compound that mistake by crying about it.

The door behind her opened and her chin tightened. She was not going to allow Zeke to guess how much she was hurting. Her face a mask of cool composure, she turned. But the mask almost slipped when she saw him. He had pulled on a pair of jeans. He'd managed to get the zipper up, but hadn't had the strength to close the snap. His skin looked flushed from his fever and his eyes were glassy. "You should be in bed," she said in a voice that made the statement an order.

"I want to apologize," he replied gruffly, leaning against the doorjamb. He raked a hand through his tousled hair and frowned as if he was having trouble focusing his thoughts. "I didn't mean to sound ungrateful for your help. Guess I've gotten a little stubborn about being self-reliant."

Suddenly terrified he might begin to guess how much she had begun to care for him, she said levelly, "I know our marriage isn't conventional. But I'd like to think we can be friends. And you don't walk out on a friend when he needs help."

"Friends," he conceded, with a nod of agreement. Then grimacing with pain, he closed his eyes.

And that is all you will ever be to him, she told herself tersely. *And you'd better keep that firmly in mind.* Aloud she said, "Now go back to bed."

His mouth twisted in a self-conscious scowl, as he opened his eyes. "I'd like to do that, but I'm a bit dizzy. I'm going to need some help from a friend to get back up those stairs."

Approaching him, she slipped his arm around her neck and her arm around his waist. "It's a wonder you didn't fall down them and break your neck," she muttered admonishingly.

"A good friend wouldn't scold a sick friend," he returned dryly.

"She would if the sick friend refused to follow the doctor's advice," she retaliated. *And if she cared as much as I do,* she added to herself.

"If you'll stop scowling at me, I'll behave from now on," he promised contritely.

Meg drew a shaky breath. She wanted to hold him and protect him forever. "Come on, cowboy," she said in gentler tones, and acting as a human crutch, she helped him back to bed.

As she handed him a couple of aspirin and a glass of water, he glanced toward the window. "Bob needs to know I can't help today and maybe you should call Jess to come over."

"I've already talked to Bob and told him to call Jess if he wanted help with any of the chores," she informed him. "You don't have to worry about a thing." Her gaze narrowed on him. "Now go to sleep."

"Yes, ma'am," he replied, and closed his eyes.

Back down in the kitchen, she made herself some coffee. "Friends is not a bad way to start," she mused philosophically. *Just don't go getting your hopes up that he'll ever allow himself to feel closer to you than that,* her inner voice warned. "I won't," she promised.

Chapter Thirteen

To her relief, Zeke followed Meg's and the doctor's orders during the next couple of days and by Sunday he was feeling much better. His fever was gone and his appetite was back.

"You make a real good cattle herder," he said as they decorated the tree Sunday evening. "Don't think I ever thanked you properly for your help." Leaning toward her, he kissed her gently.

Meg flushed with pleasure. He was in a mellow mood and she was finding it dangerously disconcerting. The temptation to allow herself to believe he might learn to care for her someday was strong. *You know better than that. Think friends,* she ordered herself.

"You're supposed to say something nice about me now," he prodded with a boyish grin as he hung a glass ball on a high branch.

The urge to wrap her arms around him and tell him how special she thought he was was strong. But she knew she couldn't do that without the danger of him guessing how much she had learned to care for him. *And he's not interested in that kind of complication in our relationship,* she reminded herself. Teasingly she looked at him as if this request required a great deal of thought. "When you want to, you can be very reasonable," she said at last.

Laying aside the decoration he had been going to hang, he drew her into his arms. "That was not particularly flattering." He scowled at her playfully. "I have half a mind not to tell you about the Christmas present I have arranged for us."

She stared up at him dubiously. "You *arranged* a Christmas present for us?"

"I didn't have much to do lying alone in bed all day long for the past couple of days," he said, leaning forward and kissing the hollow below her ear. "So I made a few phone calls."

His breath was playing havoc on the sensitive skin of her neck, making it difficult for her to think. "You were supposed to be resting and recovering." She intended for the statement to come out as an admonition, instead there was a breathless catch in her voice.

"It doesn't take much energy to make a phone call," he replied, lifting his head and placing a light kiss on the tip of her nose.

He was smiling down at her, and the softness in his eyes was causing her legs to feel weak. *Maybe he could learn to love me,* she thought wistfully. *Careful,* she warned herself in the next instant. Suddenly afraid of where her fantasies might lead her, she forced herself to concentrate on their conversation. "What have you arranged?"

"We're going on a belated honeymoon," he replied, kissing each corner of her mouth in turn, "to Jamaica."

She stared at him. "Jamaica?" He had promised her a honeymoon, but she hadn't expected anything so exotic or so romantic. Maybe this marriage was beginning to mean something deeper to him than a mere business arrangement. She smiled happily. "When?"

"December twenty-sixth through December thirtieth." His expression became serious as he lifted his head and looked down into her face. "I promised you a honeymoon. Besides, I wanted a way to thank you more fully for taking care of me while I was sick. I know I was a little difficult."

The smile on her face suddenly felt plastic. He was qualifying the trip. He didn't want her misinterpreting his actions. "It sounds like fun," she said around the lump that formed in her throat. *You were hoping for the impossible,* she chided herself. *That should teach you a lesson. If you know what's good for you, you will continue to think "friends" and forget any fantasies you might have about him learning to love you.*

* * *

"The problem with fantasies is that they don't die easily," she mused unhappily the next morning. As usual, now that they were back to their regular schedule, she had awakened alone in bed. Reaching over, she touched Zeke's pillow and found herself wishing he, at the very least, cared enough to want to say good morning to her before he started his day. "No sense dwelling on what isn't and won't be," she ordered herself, and pushing the wishful thought out of her mind, she climbed out of bed.

Later, as she went downstairs, she promised herself she wouldn't stand staring out the kitchen window trying to see him, either. She'd been stupid enough to fall in love with him. She wasn't going to compound it by acting foolishly romantic. But as she pushed open the kitchen door, she froze momentarily. Zeke was sitting at the table drinking a cup of coffee and going over his latest lesson.

"I thought you would be out doing chores somewhere," she said, with forced casualness, as she continued into the room.

"I got done what was necessary," he replied, rising and approaching her. "The rest can wait. I've been thinking that a husband and wife should have breakfast together on a regular basis."

Her heart started beating double-time. "It does sound like a nice way to start the day." *Take it slow,* she ordered herself. *Don't go letting yourself believe he cares more than he really does.* But that was easier said than done.

The next weekend he took her into Kansas City to one of the larger department stores. It had a "Get Away to the Sun" clothing department, and he insisted on buying her several outfits.

"You're spoiling me," she said with a shy smile as they drove back home.

Reaching over, he gently stroked her cheek. "You spoiled me when I was sick. It's a fair exchange."

And you'd better keep in mind that he means exactly that, she warned herself. *A kindness for a kindness is how he views what he's doing. It goes no deeper.*

Then Christmas came. She hadn't been certain what to buy for him and had settled for a couple of new shirts and a copy of *Moby Dick*. "At the rate you're learning to read, you should be ready to start on it soon," she said when he opened the package.

He thanked her with a kiss and handed her a small, elegantly wrapped gift. There was a jeweler's box inside. Opening it, she found a small emerald-and-diamond pendant on a gold chain. "It's beautiful," she said, fingering it nervously. She couldn't stop herself from thinking that it was the kind of gift a man would give the woman he loved.

"I thought the stone matched your eyes." Cupping her chin in his hand, he tilted her face upward and kissed her lightly.

A warm glow filled her. He had actually said something romantic to her. "I will treasure this gift," she said shakily.

His smile broadened. "This arrangement has worked out much better than I thought was possible."

Meg's heart froze. *You idiot!* she chided herself. She'd almost let herself believe he'd learned to care for her.

As long as he's happy, I should be happy, she told herself later that night, as she lay beside him. *Just take each day as it comes, and don't expect more than what you bargained for.* Taking a deep breath, she promised herself she would follow that advice.

By the time she drifted into a restless sleep, she honestly thought she had her fantasies under control. But the next day as they boarded their plane for Jamaica she couldn't help wishing that this was a real honeymoon, that they were two people in love. Trying to be philosophical, she told herself that she and Zeke probably had a better chance to making their marriage last than most other honeymooners. Still the fact that he didn't love her and never would caused a twist of pain. Along with this thought came the nagging worry that he would eventually get bored with her and want out of the marriage.

I will deal with that if and when it happens, she told herself. *In the meantime, I just have to keep a realistic view of our marriage and always remember that this possibility exists.*

As the plane started its descent to Montego Bay, her hands gripped the armrest. The landing strip began at the water's edge. To reach it the plane flew so low over the ocean, she was afraid it was skimming the water with the landing gear.

Zeke's hand closed over hers reassuringly. "At least the water will be warm if we have to swim for shore," he whispered in her ear.

She glanced toward him. She hadn't expected him to be paying enough attention to her to notice her nervousness. *Don't overreact and start thinking he's being extra attentive,* she scolded herself. *You probably turned as white as a sheet. A person three aisles away would have noticed.* But his touch gave her a feeling of security and drawing a deep breath, she relaxed.

Their hotel was a few miles south of Montego Bay. As their driver careened along the narrow two-lane highway, Meg again sought the security of Zeke's touch. Slipping her hand into his, she said self-consciously, "I can't get used to driving on the wrong side of the road."

He simply smiled and increased the pressure of his hold.

Don't get too used to turning to Zeke for security, she warned herself. Still she let her hand remain in his. She liked the feel of his strong fingers and his calloused palm, and she didn't see any reason to give up this small pleasure.

Their hotel was adjacent to the ocean. Walking out onto the balcony, Meg looked down at the patio area. Waiters were setting the tables of the outdoor restaurant in preparation for the evening meal. Beyond the restaurant stretched a large patio area with a swim-

ming pool. The larger portion of the pool was linked
to a smaller, shallower pool by a bridged trough.
Clusters of palm trees shaded portions of the area, and
deck chairs awaited patrons who wanted to come and
lie in the sun or sit beneath a spreading palm and enjoy the tropical breezes. Meg's gaze traveled from the
patio to the narrow beach and the blue ocean beyond.
"It's like being in the middle of a picture postcard,"
she said as Zeke joined her.

"I'm glad you like it," he replied with a soft smile,
as he kissed her lightly.

During the next couple of days, Meg had a hard
time holding onto reality. No bridegroom could have
been more attentive than Zeke. They shopped, went
horseback riding, sunbathed during the afternoons,
strolled on the beach under the stars at night and made
love. They even climbed Dunn's River Falls. The climb
hadn't been exactly what Meg had expected. She
thought they would follow a path along the side of the
falls. Instead they had climbed up through the fast-
moving water. But any time she had lost her footing or
even looked as if she was going to lose it, Zeke was
there. As the days passed, she found it harder and
harder to remind herself that he might not always be
there for her....

This has truly been a perfect honeymoon, she
thought as they followed their guide to Rose Hall. It
was their last day in Jamaica, and other guests at the
hotel had told them that they shouldn't miss seeing the
old plantation house. It was not far from the hotel in

which they were staying, and they had opted for the walking tour. Their talkative Jamaican guide stopped at each flowering plant and tree to give a short botanical lecture. But Meg was only half aware of what he was saying. What she was most aware of was that Zeke was holding her hand. When they first arrived in Jamaica, he would simply walk beside her. Now he held her hand whenever they were strolling side by side. It was a little thing, but it was beginning to give her hope that he might learn to care for her. She kept warning herself that she was putting too much emphasis on this small gesture, still she could not make herself ignore it.

When they reached the house, their walking-tour guide turned them over to a young Jamaican female who would take them through the house. But as the young woman began to tell the story of Anne Palmer, the most famous mistress of Rose Hall, Meg wished they had skipped this attraction. Anne Palmer had murdered each of her three husbands and had finally been murdered by her lover.

"I've always known love could be dangerous," Zeke remarked as they left the house and strolled back to the hotel.

The hope that had begun to grow in Meg died a swift death. "I doubt if Anne Palmer knew the meaning of the word," she said stiffly.

"But her husbands and lover were in love with her and look what happened to them," he pointed out.

"One-sided love can be very dangerous," she agreed wholeheartedly. Zeke was holding her hand again, but this time his touch carried no feeling of security. *Because their is none with him,* she reminded herself curtly. *And I'd better not forget that.*

Two days later she again found herself thinking that one-sided love could be very dangerous. She and Zeke were attending a large New Year's Eve dance being held as a fund-raiser by the local Rotary club. Kate was there with them.

"I can't believe Rita would have the nerve to show up dressed like that," Kate said with disgust, as several wolf whistles sounded from near the door.

Twisting in her seat, Meg saw the redhead coming in. She was wearing a black sequined dress that fitted her like a second skin. The neckline was cut low, and a slit along the side of the floor-length skirt ran upward to the very top of her thigh, exposing the entire length of her leg.

Spotting Zeke, Rita waved and came toward their table with Frank following behind. "I really can't believe you two went to Jamaica," she said, flashing Zeke a bright smile. "Frank..." she glanced toward her husband and her mouth formed a petulant pout, "...has never taken me any place more exotic than the zoo."

Frank shifted uneasily. "Think I need a drink," he said. "Come on, Rita."

But Rita didn't move. "You go get us drinks," she said, her voice a soft purr. "I want to visit a moment longer."

Meg wondered if her skin was as green as her eyes. Even if Zeke felt no deep emotional bonds with Rita, as a man he had to be attracted to her. *Jealousy is a very destructive emotion,* she warned herself, determined to keep it under control.

"You don't mind if I borrow Zeke for one little dance for old time's sake?" Rita was saying, as the band began playing a slow melody. As she spoke, she wrapped her hands around Zeke's arm and gently urged him to leave his chair.

"I really don't think that's such a good idea," Zeke said, refusing to rise.

Meg couldn't help noting that he didn't say he didn't want to dance with the woman. He'd simply said it wasn't a good idea.

"Meg won't mind," Rita insisted, continuing to pull on his arm. She leaned further toward him, exposing more breast.

Meg felt the bile rise in her throat. She wanted to scream at Rita to let go of Zeke, but instead she forced herself to maintain a calm facade.

Rita turned her gaze toward Meg and a malicious gleam sparkled in her eyes. "You don't mind if Zeke and I take a little turn around the floor, do you?" she asked in honey-coated tones.

Meg bit back a sharp *yes.* "Of course not," she replied, then flinched when Kate gave her a swift kick under the table.

With a triumphant smile, Rita turned her attention back to Zeke. "Come on," she insisted.

With an indifferent shrug, Zeke rose.

"I can't believe you're allowing this," Kate scolded in lowered tones, as she and Meg watched the couple walk to the dance floor. "Rumor has it that Rita and Frank are going to split again, and it looks to me that she's getting ready to set her cap for your husband."

Meg's stomach knotted. "I can't tell Zeke what to do or not to do," she replied, trying not to show any of the hurt or anger she was feeling because he hadn't continued to refuse to dance with the woman.

"He's your husband. You're supposed to fight for him," Kate persisted.

Meg was barely listening. Her hands were balled into fists, as she fought to retain control of her anger and jealousy. Rita and Zeke had reached the dance floor, and as they began to move to the music, Rita molded herself against Zeke's sturdy form.

Kate gave Meg a sharp nudge. "You've got to do something. People are watching." Kate nodded toward the bar, and her voice took on an even more urgent note. "And Frank's getting drunk. That can only mean trouble, if you don't do something now."

But Meg was barely listening to her mother. She was watching Rita whisper in Zeke's ear. Her control snapped. He was still her husband, and she wasn't going to sit there and be made to look like a fool. Rising, she walked with dignity to the couple and tapped Rita on the shoulder.

"Sorry, no cutting in on this dance," the redhead said with a seductive giggle, continuing to hold onto Zeke even though he had come to a halt.

Meg stared at her icily. "If you are so anxious to make a spectacle of yourself, go do it with someone else's husband."

Rita tossed her a caustic glance. "Zeke is only yours by default." Returning her attention to Zeke, a wistful, seductiveness played over her features. "And I'm beginning to think I made a terrible mistake."

He scowled down at her. "Then you'll have to live with it," he said grimly, freeing the hand she was holding and removing her other hand from his shoulder. He nodded toward the bar. "Your husband could use a little looking after." Before Rita could say more, Zeke had swept Meg up in his arms and was guiding her across the dance floor. "I was wondering if you were going to rescue me before Frank decided to take a swing at me," he said in her ear, as those who had been watching now returned to minding their own business.

"You could have avoided having to worry about Frank if you'd refused to dance with her in the first place," Meg replied coolly, still smarting from the mental image of Zeke and Rita in one another's arms.

He regarded her dryly. "You practically told me to dance with her."

"I did not!" she snapped, furious that he would try to lay the blame for his behavior on her. "I simply didn't make the decision for you." Her voice took on a sarcastic edge. "You're a big boy. I assumed you knew how to avoid trouble."

"So did I," he muttered.

Her body tensed. She didn't want to say what was on her mind, but she had never been one to avoid the truth. "Maybe you're getting bored with your life as it is at the moment," she suggested stiffly.

Releasing her hand, he captured her chin and tilted her face upward. There was a heat in the dark brown depths of his eyes that took her breath away. "I am definitely not bored."

Relief washed over her. "I am glad," she admitted honestly. Although she was still worried their marriage wouldn't last, she wasn't ready for it to end so soon.

Smiling, he kissed her as the music stopped.

"Well that should show Rita where she stands," Kate said, beaming happily when Meg and Zeke returned to the table.

Meg's heart was still racing. It took so little from Zeke, a touch or even a look, to cause her body to come alive with desire. *I just hope I can continue to remember where I stand,* she thought frantically.

Chapter Fourteen

"**I** swear, you seem to actually have a glow about you." Kate smiled brightly at Meg, as the two of them sat at the table in Kate's kitchen drinking a late-afternoon cup of coffee.

It was the beginning of February. Meg had stopped by to visit with her mother for a few minutes before going home at the end of the school day. "I'm enjoying married life," she confessed. *A little too much,* her inner voice added, but she ignored it. She had decided to live each day as it came and not worry about the future. She loved Zeke and she was going to enjoy what time she had with him.

Kate was still watching her daughter closely. "You're pregnant."

Meg shook her head. "No." What amazed her was that she hadn't even been disappointed this morning when her body let her know she was not yet going to have a baby. Just being with Zeke was enough to make her happy.

"Well, I am glad to see this marriage of yours has worked out so well," Kate said, reaching over and giving her daughter's hand a squeeze.

A knock sounded on the back door. Glancing toward its lace-covered window, Meg saw Lucile Tate standing there.

"I hate to interrupt your visit with Meg," Lucile said apologetically when Kate opened the door. Moving like a woman with a purpose, she barely gave Kate time to step aside before she entered. Not even pausing to remove her coat, she marched toward the table. "But I thought she should know."

"Know what?" Meg asked. There was a definite set to Lucile's jaw that warned Meg she was not going to like what she heard.

"Rita and Frank are getting a divorce," Lucile announced with the aplomb of a town crier.

"Rita and Frank are always either getting divorced or getting married," Kate interjected sarcastically.

The frown on Lucile's face deepened. "This time it's different. The time Rita says it's for good." Lucile shifted her weight as if she was suddenly very uncomfortable. "Maybe I shouldn't have come over." Turning abruptly, she started toward the door.

Meg was on her feet in an instant. She'd never known Lucile Tate to stop in the middle of a bit of gossip. Moving toward the door, she blocked the woman's exit. "You're here. You might as well tell me everything."

"Rita is going around town saying that Zeke was in love with her, and married you on the rebound when she went back to Frank. She says she knows she made a mistake. Zeke is the man she wants and she intends to get him back," Lucile blurted out.

Inwardly Meg felt as if someone had punched her hard in the stomach, but outwardly she maintained an air of calm. "Rita likes to hear herself talk."

Lucile nodded. "That's what I told everyone," she said. "I told them that you and Zeke had a solid marriage."

About as solid as soup, Meg thought. Outwardly, however, she maintained a confident manner. Thanking Lucile for the information, she stepped out of the way, opened the door and allowed the woman to leave.

"Well, what are you going to do?" Kate asked as soon as she and Meg were alone.

"I don't know," Meg answered honestly.

Kate studied her daughter worriedly. "Do you think there's any truth in what Rita is claiming?"

"Zeke told me he didn't love her," she replied. He'd also told her he never lied. But she couldn't help wondering if he was lying to himself. His proposal to her had been unexpected and had followed almost immediately on the heels of Rita's marriage. And even if he wasn't in love with the woman, she would be a temptation to any man. "I should be going home," she said, pulling on her coat.

Kate gave her daughter a tight hug. "I'll be here if you need me."

Meg's stomach was in knots by the time she reached the farm.

"I was beginning to worry about you," Zeke said, coming into the hall to greet her.

She avoided his eyes as she took off her coat and hung it in the closet. "I stopped by to see Mom for a few minutes after school."

Taking her in his arms, he kissed her on the tip of her nose. "How is Kate?"

"She's fine," she replied, fighting the urge to wrap her arms around him as tightly as she could and never let go. Forcing herself to meet his gaze, she said levelly, "Lucile Tate came over to tell us that Rita and Frank are getting a divorce."

"I'm beginning to believe those two enjoy fighting." He kissed her lightly on the mouth. "As for me, I prefer our arrangement."

You don't know how much I want to believe that, Meg thought frantically, wrapping her arms around his neck and adding her own strength to the kiss.

But during the next few days she couldn't help noticing Zeke seemed uneasy. It wasn't anything she could put her finger on. It was just a feeling she had.

On Wednesday of the next week, he went into Kansas City for the day. He didn't tell her he was going.

Afterward, it occurred to her that she might never have known about the trip except that he got back later than he expected to.

He wasn't at the farm when she came home from work that day. Wondering if she should start dinner or wait a while, she'd asked Bob where Zeke had gone.

"Don't rightly know. He's been off running an errand all day. Didn't say where he was going but he was expecting to be back before now," Bob told her with a mildly worried look on his face. "Ain't like him to disappear for so long without telling someone where he's going."

Meg kept her expression nonchalant. "I'm sure he'll show up soon," she said and went inside. But once she was alone, her jaw tensed. In the living room, she paced the floor, her thoughts vacillating between being worried sick that Zeke had been in an accident and wondering if maybe his errand had involved a certain shapely redhead.

Zeke showed up a few minutes after Meg had started her pacing. He wasn't dressed in his usual faded jeans and work shirt. Instead he was wearing a pair of dress slacks and one of his good shirts. "Sorry I wasn't here when you got home," he apologized, greeting her with a kiss. "Had to go into Kansas City on business. Took longer than I thought it would."

She waited for a fuller explanation, but he didn't give any. Instead he kissed her again, then asked what was for dinner. "Chicken," she replied, noting that the uneasiness she'd sensed in him during the past few days was gone. She told herself that they didn't have the kind of relationship where they pried into one another's business. But if Zeke had cheated on her, that was her business, she argued back. "Was your trip successful?" she asked.

"Worked out fine," he replied in an easy drawl. Without giving her time to probe further, he headed for the stairs. "Need to change and check on a few things before dinner," he said over his shoulder. "Want to make certain Bob moved those cows."

"He'll tell me about his day at dinner," she assured herself firmly. Although Joan had come back, Meg was still doing a great deal of Zeke's bookkeeping. During dinner each evening, he'd begun to talk openly to her about the business he was conducting or even thinking of conducting.

But that night, he didn't mention the trip to Kansas City. He talked about the farm and some future plans he had for it, but Kansas City was never mentioned.

Finally Meg could stand it no longer. "You haven't mentioned why you had to go into Kansas City today," she said with forced casualness.

He shrugged as if to say the trip hadn't been important. "Had something I needed to check up on," he replied. Leaning toward her, he traced the line of her jaw with his fingertip. "How about if we clean these dishes up later," he suggested, kissing her invitingly.

If he was purposely evading her question, he certainly had a very effective method, she thought as her whole body warmed beneath the heat of his gaze.

Gently he massaged the taut cords of her neck until her toes curled with pleasure. "I've got the logs ready to be lit for a fire in the living room," he said huskily, nibbling on her earlobe.

She wanted to resist him, wanted to insist that he tell her what he had been doing in Kansas City. Tersely she reminded herself that she didn't have that right. His business was his business unless he chose to share it with her. His mouth found hers and the persuasive touch of his lips melted all thoughts of resistance.

When he rose, she rose. And when he lifted her in his arms and carried her into the living room, she let herself push all thoughts of Kansas City to the far corner of her mind.

But during the next days, they came back to nag at her. She couldn't help wondering if his uneasiness had really been restlessness, and if he had spent the day with Rita to quell it. But she refused to believe that he had. Zeke was a man of his word, and he had promised to be faithful to her for as long as they were married. Besides he hadn't acted guilty. What really hurt was that he had shut her out. It was a little thing, but it made it clear that he was as determined as ever to maintain a separateness between them.

Ordering herself not to think about the Kansas City trip any more, Meg glanced at the calendar. It was February fourteenth. Valentine's Day. A bittersweet smile played across her face. It was a day for people in love. "Not the kind of holiday Zeke is going to pay much attention to," she muttered as she went downstairs.

But as she opened the kitchen door, a lump rose in her throat. Zeke was sitting at the table, drinking a cup of coffee and waiting for her. In the middle of the table there was a vase filled with a dozen long-stemmed red roses and a huge heart-shaped box of candy.

For a moment she stood in the door unable to move.

"You're not allergic to roses, are you?" he questioned teasingly, standing up.

"No, I'm not allergic," she managed, continuing into the room. "I'm just surprised. They're beautiful."

He continued to regard her with amusement. "I thought it was traditional for husbands to give their wives flowers and candy on Valentine's Day."

"Yes, it is," she conceded shakily.

"And isn't also traditional for the husband to receive a thank-you kiss for being so generous?" he coaxed.

"Very definitely," she replied. Approaching him, she circled her arms around his neck, and rising up on tiptoes, kissed him. But when she started to release him and step away, he tightened his hold on her.

"I was very generous," he said, nodding toward the candy and flowers.

There was a warmth in the dark depths of his eyes that could have melted the polar ice cap, and he was bantering with her as if they were lovers who were truly in love. Meg's heart began to pound erratically. "Yes, you were very generous," she agreed. Her arms again fastened around his neck and her lips sought his for a second time. As the kiss deepened, her body molded to his. She wanted to stay in his arms forever. Deserting his mouth, she trailed kisses to the hollow of his neck. She loved the masculine smell of him and the salty taste of his skin.

"We'd better stop this now," he warned huskily, releasing her. "Or you're going to be late for school."

Meg groaned at being freed. "I would like to play hooky with you," she said wistfully. Then flushed self-consciously at the openness of her admission.

"Why, Margaret Wilson, I can't believe I am hearing those words from you," he teased, giving her a light pat on the seat. "Sit down and have some breakfast. You can thank me more thoroughly when you get home. I don't want to rush this. After all, I was very, very generous."

"Very, very," she conceded, wishing they could continue the "thank you" right now. But Zeke was already at the stove, breaking eggs into the skillet.

Later as she drove to school, she couldn't stop smiling. She kept remembering the warmth in his eyes. And there were the roses and the candy. She hadn't expected him to even remember it was Valentine's Day. She knew it was dangerous, but she couldn't stop herself from again beginning to hope that he might be learning to care for her.

"My mother says Ted is up to something," Gale Gytha, the principal's secretary, was saying worriedly to Barbara Bradley as Meg entered the office to check her mailbox before school started.

Meg knew Gale was talking about Ted Randall, her latest boyfriend. Meg also knew that Ted was not exactly what a person could describe as the sincere type. Whatever Gale's mother's suspicions were, they were probably right.

"Mom says it's natural for a man to bring a woman a box of candy or a dozen roses for Valentine's Day," Gale continued in anxious tones. "Or he might even bring her one rose and a box of candy. But if he brings a huge box of candy and a dozen roses, he's probably feeling guilty about something. And that's just what Ted showed up with, on my doorstep this morning, when he came to drive me to work."

Meg's knuckles whitened around the handle of her briefcase. Again she found herself wondering about Zeke's trip to Kansas City.

"Maybe your Ted is a little more generous than most men. I wouldn't jump to any conclusions," Barbara said in soothing tones. She glanced toward Meg. "Don't you agree, Meg?"

"That's certainly possible," Meg managed to say around the lump forming in her throat. Not wanting to get caught in the middle of a discussion about Ted and Gale's relationship, she added quickly, "I've got to get going. See you two later."

Escaping to the solitude of her classroom, she noticed her hands were shaking. Going over to the window, she opened it and took several deep breaths. She tried to put the conversation in the office out of her mind. But all morning, thoughts of Zeke, the candy and flowers, and his trip to Kansas City tormented her. By noon, she admitted that it didn't matter if Gale's mother was right or wrong in her assessment of the size and portion of Valentine's Day gifts. What mattered was that she, Margaret Delany Wilson, couldn't go on like this any longer... allowing her hopes to build one minute, then seeing them crushed the next. It was time to face the truth. Zeke was always going to keep her on the fringe of his life. His unwillingness to discuss his Kansas City trip proved that. Even more to the point, he would always keep her shut out of his heart. It hurt too much to go on like this.

Driving home... back to Zeke's farm... she corrected herself, she worked on building up her courage. She knew what she had to do, but just the thought of it caused her stomach to twist into knots.

When Zeke came out to meet her with a warm smile on his face, her resolve almost crumbled. His arms looked so inviting.

Don't let him touch you, she warned herself curtly. "We have to talk," she said stiffly, skirting him and walking briskly into the house.

Catching up with her in the hall, his hand closed around her arm bringing her to an abrupt halt. "What's happened?" he demanded, studying her worriedly. "This morning you were all warm and tender. Now you act as if you can't stand the thought of me touching you."

The heat from his hand was spreading through her. Hot tears burned at the back of her eyes. This was going to be even harder than she had imagined. "I know this may seem sudden, but it's for the best," she said tightly. A huge lump formed in her throat. It took every ounce of control to swallow it back and say what she knew she had to say. "I've decided that this marriage isn't working. I want out."

Shock followed by anger flashed in Zeke's eyes. Then they became shuttered. "I know you're unhappy about not being pregnant yet," he said stiffly. "But I'm perfectly capable of siring the children you want. That's why I went to Kansas City. I went to see a specialist to make certain I could keep my part of our bargain." His jaw tensed further. "Sometimes you just have to give nature a little time to work."

So that was why he had gone to Kansas City. A part of her was relieved to learn she had been right and that it hadn't been to see Rita. But that doesn't really make any difference, she told herself curtly. He'd referred to their marriage as a bargain. That was all it would ever be to him, and that fact was tearing her apart inside. "I've never questioned your ability to father children," she said levelly. "I just can't go on with this marriage."

For a moment his hold on her arm tightened. Then with tense control, he released her. "We did agree that if either one of us wanted out all we had to do was ask," he said. A cynical smile played across his mouth. "Consider yourself free."

Her throat too constricted to speak, Meg nodded. *Fool!* she chided herself when she realized that she had hoped, down deep inside, that he wouldn't agree so easily. She wanted to run up the stairs to their bedroom to pack, but instead she forced herself to walk with quiet dignity. *This is the way it has to be,* she told herself as she retrieved her large suitcase from a closet in the spare room and carried it into the room she had shared with Zeke. She didn't have the strength to pack everything. She'd just take what she needed for now and send her mother for the rest.

The tears begged to flow, but she held them back. She couldn't let him see her cry. Unsnapping the suitcase, she began to throw clothes into it haphazardly. She had to get out of here as fast as possible.

Suddenly Zeke's large bulk filled the doorway. "Why, Meg? Just for the record, I'd like to know," he demanded grimly. "I've treated you well. I know I haven't always been easy to get along with, but I've tried."

Looking up she saw the anger behind the guarded expression on his face. A part of her wanted to think his question was because he cared, but she knew it was only his pride that needed the answer. "It isn't you," she replied, shakily. "It's me." Unable to face him any longer, she turned away to gather another armload of clothes.

Zeke's expression grew grimmer. "That's not an answer, Meg. I want to know why you're leaving."

She didn't have the strength to fight him. She wanted him to go away and she felt certain the truth would send him running. Her chin threatened to tremble when she again raised her head to meet his narrowed steady gaze, but she held it firm. "Because I did something really stupid . . . really, really stupid." She spread her hands in a gesture of helplessness. "I fell in love with you."

The scowl on his face deepened. "You're not making any sense. If you love me, why won't you stay?" he questioned harshly.

Turning away from him, she walked over to the window and looked out at the barren winter landscape. "I told myself I could handle it if the time ever came when you grew bored with me and wanted your freedom." A bitter smile tilted one corner of her mouth. "But the truth is, if I stay here any longer, I don't think I can. I tried to stop, but I keep loving you more with each passing day." Her voice threatened to break. "I never thought anything could hurt this much." Hot tears were burning at the back of her eyes. But she had her pride. She couldn't bear the thought of crying in front of him. She had to get away before she made a complete fool of herself. Turning, she strode toward the bureau and grabbing another armload of clothes threw them into the suitcase. But as she turned back toward the dresser, Zeke blocked her path.

"I don't want you to leave, Meg," he said gruffly.

The anguish on his face caused her breath to lock in her lungs. Maybe he did care for her.

"We have a good arrangement," he finished tersely.

Idiot! she cursed herself. "Please, just go away and let me pack in peace," she requested through clenched teeth.

But he refused to move. "You gave me your word you would teach me to read and to do my own books."

Damn! Didn't he understand how much this was hurting her? "You're learning to read at an extremely rapid rate. I'm sure you can work out some arrangement with Norma Royd and Joan will stick around until you can take over the bookkeeping," she replied stiffly.

"What about the children you want?" he questioned curtly.

"I'll get a dog or a cat. That's what I should have done in the first place." The tears burned hotter at the back of her eyes. She had to get out of here.

She started around him, but his hands closed like steel bars around her arms. "Meg, please, stay. You've made this place feel like a home. You've given it warmth."

She couldn't look at him. The urge to give in to his request was too strong. *He only wants a warm body in his bed and a companion to talk to when he's bored,* she reminded herself curtly. "I'm sure you can find any number of women to suit your requirements," she replied. She studied the middle button on his shirt. "Now, please let go of me and let me get out of here."

Very slowly he released her. "No one will ever suit me as well as you," he said gruffly, shoving his hands into the pockets of his jeans as he stepped out of her way.

She could feel him watching her gather up a final armload of clothes and drop them haphazardly into the suitcase. As she snapped the suitcase shut, she suddenly found herself worrying about who was going to take care of him when he was sick. *He took care of himself just fine before you came along,* she reminded herself tersely. Panic filled her. She wanted to stay so badly it was a physical pain. *Get out of here before you do something else really stupid,* she commanded herself. Picking up the suitcase, she started toward the door.

"Meg," Zeke said her name with a gruff plea.

Don't look back, she ordered herself. *Keep walking.*

"I love you, Meg."

She froze. Maybe she wanted to hear him say those words so badly, she'd imagined it. Very slowly she turned to face him. "What did you say?" she asked levelly.

"I said that I love you," he replied.

Her chin trembled. "You wouldn't lie to me, would you?"

He was watching her grimly. "I told you before, I never lie."

She studied him uncertainly. "You don't have to make it sound like a curse."

"I've spent a lot of years keeping people at arm's length." A self-mocking smile played at the corners of his mouth. "I figured this arrangement of ours would be perfect. It was practical and sensible. I found you physically attractive, but I thought you were emotionally frosty. That suited me just fine." He drew a breath. "The problem was, you weren't frosty. You weren't even chilly. You were warm and giving. I liked having you around. I liked talking to you. I liked making love to you. It scared me when I realized how much you were beginning to mean to me. I admit I fought it, but it was a losing battle." He looked at her beseechingly. "I know I'm not the easiest man to get along with, but will you stay with me, Meg?"

His barriers were down. He looked so vulnerable standing there waiting for her to answer she wanted to run into his arms, but her legs felt like putty. "I think you're supposed to kiss a girl after you've told her that you love her," she said, letting her suitcase drop to the floor.

Relief shown on his face. In three long strides he reached her. "That sure sounds like the right thing to do," he agreed. Drawing her into his embrace, his lips sought hers with a kiss that promised forever.

She wanted to laugh and cry at the same time. It felt so good being held by him and knowing that he wanted her in his arms and no one else. So much for Gale's mother's theories, she mused as a joy she had never felt before spread over her. "Happy Valentine's Day," she murmured when he deserted her mouth to nibble on her earlobe.

His hands moved possessively along the curves of her body. Lifting his head, he frowned playfully into her face. "That reminds me. I believe you owe me a thank you."

Her body ignited beneath his touch. "A very big thank you," she confirmed, kissing the hollow of his neck as she began to work the buttons of his shirt open.

* * * * *

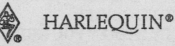
HARLEQUIN®

Don't miss these Harlequin favorites by some of our most distinguished authors!
And now, you can receive a discount by ordering two or more titles!

HT #25645	THREE GROOMS AND A WIFE by JoAnn Ross	$3.25 U.S./$3.75 CAN. ☐
HT #25648	JESSIE'S LAWMAN by Kristine Rolofson	$3.25 U.S.//$3.75 CAN. ☐
HP #11725	THE WRONG KIND OF WIFE by Roberta Leigh	$3.25 U.S./$3.75 CAN. ☐
HP #11755	TIGER EYES by Robyn Donald	$3.25 U.S./$3.75 CAN. ☐
HR #03362	THE BABY BUSINESS by Rebecca Winters	$2.99 U.S./$3.50 CAN. ☐
HR #03375	THE BABY CAPER by Emma Goldrick	$2.99 U.S./$3.50 CAN. ☐
HS #70638	THE SECRET YEARS by Margot Dalton	$3.75 U.S./$4.25 CAN. ☐
HS #70655	PEACEKEEPER by Marisa Carroll	$3.75 U.S./$4.25 CAN. ☐
HI #22280	MIDNIGHT RIDER by Laura Pender	$2.99 U.S./$3.50 CAN. ☐
HI #22235	BEAUTY VS THE BEAST by M.J. Rogers	$3.50 U.S./$3.99 CAN. ☐
HAR #16531	TEDDY BEAR HEIR by Elda Minger	$3.50 U.S./$3.99 CAN. ☐
HAR #16596	COUNTERFEIT HUSBAND by Linda Randall Wisdom	$3.50 U.S./$3.99 CAN. ☐
HH #28795	PIECES OF SKY by Marianne Willman	$3.99 U.S./$4.50 CAN. ☐
HH #28855	SWEET SURRENDER by Julie Tetel	$4.50 U.S./$4.99 CAN. ☐

(limited quantities available on certain titles)

	AMOUNT	$
DEDUCT:	10% DISCOUNT FOR 2+ BOOKS	$
ADD:	POSTAGE & HANDLING	$
	($1.00 for one book, 50¢ for each additional)	
	APPLICABLE TAXES**	$_____
	TOTAL PAYABLE	$_____
	(check or money order—please do not send cash)	

To order, complete this form and send it, along with a check or money order for the total above, payable to Harlequin Books, to: **In the U.S.:** 3010 Walden Avenue, P.O. Box 9047, Buffalo, NY 14269-9047; **In Canada:** P.O. Box 613, Fort Erie, Ontario, L2A 5X3.

Name: _____

Address: _____ City: _____

State/Prov.: _____ Zip/Postal Code: _____

**New York residents remit applicable sales taxes.
  Canadian residents remit applicable GST and provincial taxes.   HBACK-AJ3

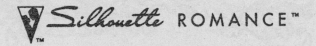

What's a single dad to do when he needs a wife by next Thursday?

Who's a confirmed bachelor to call when he finds a baby on his doorstep?

How does a plain Jane in love with her gorgeous boss get him to notice her?

From classic love stories to romantic comedies to emotional heart tuggers, **Silhouette Romance** offers six irresistible novels every month by some of your favorite authors!
Such as…beloved bestsellers **Diana Palmer,**
Annette Broadrick, Suzanne Carey, Elizabeth August and **Marie Ferrarella,** to name just a few—and some sure to become favorites!

Fabulous Fathers…Bundles of Joy…Miniseries…
Months of blushing brides and convenient weddings…
Holiday celebrations… You'll find all this and much more in
Silhouette Romance—always emotional, always enjoyable, always about love!

SR-GEN

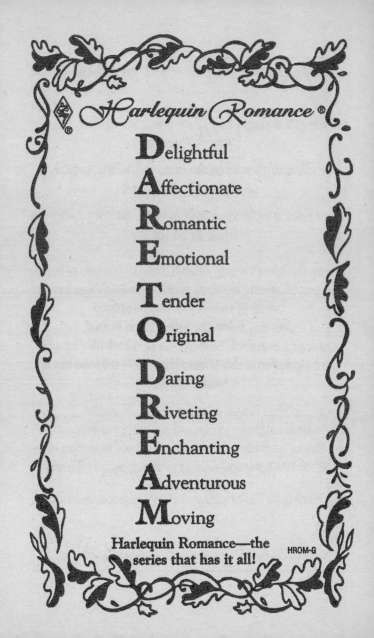

Harlequin Romance ®

Delightful

Affectionate

Romantic

Emotional

Tender

Original

Daring

Riveting

Enchanting

Adventurous

Moving

Harlequin Romance—the
series that has it all!

HROM-G

◆ Harlequin®
◆ Historical

If you're a serious fan of historical romance,
then you're in luck!

Harlequin Historicals brings you
stories by bestselling authors, rising new stars
and talented first-timers.

Ruth Langan & Theresa Michaels
Mary McBride & Cheryl St. John
Margaret Moore & Merline Lovelace
Julie Tetel & Nina Beaumont
Susan Amarillas & Ana Seymour
Deborah Simmons & Linda Castle
Cassandra Austin & Emily French
Miranda Jarrett & Suzanne Barclay
DeLoras Scott & Laurie Grant...

You'll never run out of favorites.

Harlequin Historicals...they're too good to miss!

HH-GEN

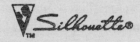

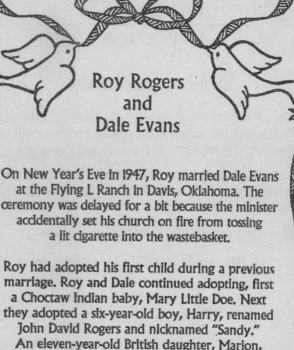

Roy Rogers
and
Dale Evans

On New Year's Eve in 1947, Roy married Dale Evans at the Flying L Ranch in Davis, Oklahoma. The ceremony was delayed for a bit because the minister accidentally set his church on fire from tossing a lit cigarette into the wastebasket.

Roy had adopted his first child during a previous marriage. Roy and Dale continued adopting, first a Choctaw Indian baby, Mary Little Doe. Next they adopted a six-year-old boy, Harry, renamed John David Rogers and nicknamed "Sandy." An eleven-year-old British daughter, Marion, came next, followed by a Korean orphan, Debbie.

Dale has written three books benefiting charities about the children they tragically lost: *Angel Unaware*, *Dearest Debbie* and *Salute to Sandy*.

B-RROGERS